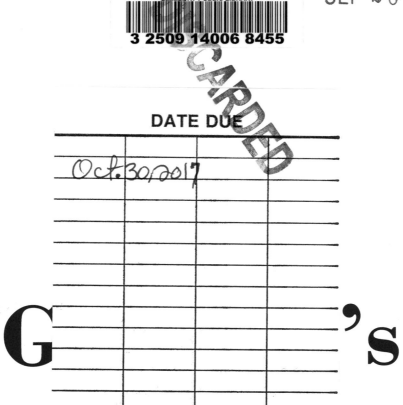

DATE DUE

Oct. 30, 2017

PRINTED IN U.S.A.

G ’s
G ne

Linda Massucci

Helping Hands Press
922 S. Woodbourne Road, Suite 153
Levittown, PA 19056

First Edition

For discounts on bulk purchases, please email
contactus@myhelpinghandspress.com

Printed in the United States of America

ISBN: 978-1-62208-572-9

Acknowledgments

During the writing process of 'Legacy of Grandpa's Grapevine', the year also included traveling across the United States to complete interviews for my first non-fiction book, 'It Had To Be You'. It was a year of life-changing opportunities and events.

Thank you to my family and friends for their unwavering support and words of wisdom. My phone calls and e-mails are always answered with positive responses and helpful advice. I am very fortunate to be blessed with a family that provides unconditional love and support. My friends always remind me to challenge myself and view everything as an opportunity to learn & grow.

'Legacy of Grandpa's Grapevine' would never be published without my agent- Diana Flegal. Thank you Diana and everyone at Hartline Agency for loving Grandpa Frank and Elizabeth as much as I do.

Thank you all and enjoy the book!

Linda Massucci

Dedication

The characters in this book are a culmination of people I have met, and a few I have created, throughout the years. The characters and events could never have been created without someone instilling a love of writing in me and the freedom to use my imagination. My memories of elementary school include kick ball games, science experiments, field trips, and teachers reading aloud while the students closed their eyes to visualize the characters. My fondest memory is in the sixth grade. Every Friday, my sixth grade teacher would hand out the writing journals. Everyone, including her, would write for sixty-minutes. There was no prompt, no score and no critiquing. We all just wrote. Some wrote stories, others wrote poems. I remember the room being so quiet you could hear the pencils rubbing on the paper. There was no time limit either. If you didn't finish your story, there was always next Friday. After all, how can you put a time limit on creativity?

It was on those Fridays that I began to realize I was good at something. I could write. So, the class-clown went from disrupting social studies class, to 'jotting down' an historical event to use in a short story. I began to view everything and everyone in my life as future characters and short stories. Many characters I created in that sixth grade class in 1983 are in the short stories and books I write today. Characters that would not have come to fruition without one teacher deciding to put aside the text and schedule for just an hour once a week, and allowing her students to write with imagination, curiosity and freedom.

Thank you, Mrs. Kalosky, my sixth grade teacher at Central Elementary in Southington, CT. You were an educator who inspired, motivated and loved her students, without ever a word of criticism or attempt to label a child as remedial, special or gifted. We were all challenges and we were all a priority. We were never, under your watch, left behind.

Linda Massucci

In memory
Grandpa Frank and Great-Grandpa Pasquale Massucci

Table of Contents

Prologue

I can't recall the first memory I have of my Grandpa Frank, but I can recall the many Sundays at his home just listening to him speak. He told stories of coming to America with ten dollars in his pocket and his best girl by his side. When he laughed, you could see his stained teeth from all those cigars he smoked since the age of twelve. His face was worn from working outside at the trolley yards and his hands had calluses and scars. Grandpa Frank was a slim man with wavy white hair. I'm sure, in his youth, he must have been an attractive man, but to me he was just my Grandpa Frank. An old man who always had time to sit with me and listen to my worries, hopes, and insecurities. Whether I was eight years old or sixteen years old, I could always depend on Grandpa Frank for a listening ear. He was never hard to find either. From my house to his, it was a quick bike ride and all downhill too! Pass the town bank, cross the street at the market, turn left across the tracks, and you entered the Italian side of town. Grandpa Frank and Grandma Marie moved into the two story white house after they left Brooklyn. Grandpa said the Italian section was called Goat's Island, because so many of the families had goats in their yards. I don't remember Grandpa Frank having goats- I guess he got too tired of taking care of them. There was one thing he never got tired of caring for, and that was his grapevine. That is where I could always find my Grandpa Frank. He loved to sit under that grapevine and smoke his cigars. He would watch the trains pass by and think out loud about where it might be going. The grapevine was his place to think about all the yesterdays, the struggles he and Grandma Marie overcame while raising a family, and maybe to ponder how many more days he would be blessed with her in his life. I always got a feeling of excitement when I saw my Grandpa Frank sitting under his grapevine. I knew whatever problems I had, he could fix with a story or words of wisdom. I had to listen carefully as he spoke in his broken English, but I didn't mind taking my time with Grandpa Frank. He always seemed so confident and brave in my eyes, why would I want to rush away from such a man. I thought, in my youth, he would always be there for me. I guess that's what makes being young so wonderful- the concept of time is not fully understood. Now, I am much older and completely understand how quickly time passes. As I drive down I-84 in Connecticut and take my hometown exit, I realize Grandpa Frank will not be waiting for me under his grapevine. As an adult, I realize death is just a part of life. As a granddaughter, I just want to sit with Grandpa Frank and ask him one more question. I guess I should have come home a lot sooner.

The Journey Home

Who would have thought I could tear myself away from all the deadlines and rewrites in the publishing world. On Tuesday morning, I received a call from my father. Grandpa Frank was not doing very well and I should take a drive to Connecticut to say goodbye. I went to work that morning to try and get all the things that can't wait done. I rescheduled my Friday interviews for a book I was working on. It would be great to leave the city for a three day weekend in Connecticut. On Wednesday morning, I called my parents and said I would be arriving on Friday. My mother was quiet on the phone. Her only response was, 'I guess if that's the soonest you could get here. Your father will tell Grandpa Frank you are coming soon.' Thursday morning, I awoke to my alarm and jumped in the shower. After I got dressed and was eating breakfast, I checked my schedule for the day. I was thinking how I could strategically move some appointments around, so I could leave Manhattan by mid-day. The phone rang. It was my mother. My Grandpa Frank had passed away in the early morning hours. I told my mother I would be home by noon.

Just off the highway, exit 32, was the place I called home. I hadn't lived there for over 15 years, the town had changed dramatically. It's funny how I couldn't wait to leave the place and find excitement and real life. There still remains a part of you that secretly hopes the place will stay the same for your own greediness and insecurities. It becomes a place that you can return to with the hopes of feeling as safe as you did in your youth. I entered my hometown of Southington. I quickly understood the saying, 'You can never go home again.' The farms were replaced with mini-malls. Traffic lights were put in place, where once only a stop sign was needed. Grandpa's trolley tracks were dismantled, and replaced with walking trails. The downtown merchants I recalled were no longer in business. The streets were lined with BMW's and a Lexus or two. Extravagant homes built, where once apple orchards stood and grazing sheep roamed.

It was a far cry from the working community I remembered. There was a local pharmacy, a department store, two grocery stores, and you really did shop downtown on Thursday night. There were small businesses with loyal customers who paid on credit, with no monthly interest. You could walk down the street and know everyone you passed, and you always said hello. If you were a kid, you better behave, because someone would see you, who knew someone, who knows your father. It was a small town....it is my hometown.

As I passed the old bank, which has since been sold to a larger bank, I just had to turn my car towards the old market, left across the tracks, and drive by my Grandparents' house. I parked in the driveway and slowly got out of my car. The house still looked the same. The windows were spotless, the house had a fresh coat of white paint, and the flower garden was immaculate. My feet traveled to the back yard. I spotted my Grandpa Frank's grapevine. It was in perfect condition, just like I always remembered. It was nice to know some things never change. Grandpa Frank could wave to all the families using the walking trail. I pictured him smoking his cigar, glass of wine in one hand, and waving to the families with the other hand. I gave a silent chuckle and then a sigh of regret. I realized Grandpa Frank wouldn't be sitting under this grapevine anymore. I would never smell his cigars again or listen to his stories with a strained ear, as he spoke in broken English.

"Elizabeth, I thought I'd find you here."

I turned and saw my father walking toward me. My father looks like the typical aging Italian man. He has wavy salt and pepper hair with a mustache that matches his hair color. He is blessed with a year round tan and always walks very straight. My father has a sort of bounce to his walk, like he has not a care in the world. My mother has said I tend to walk like this, and I'm thankful for the trait. I took a second glance at his face. It's funny how when you're away from loved ones for a period of time, they appear to have aged when you see them again. When I'm away from my folks and think about them, their faces, in my reflections, always appear young and vibrant. Now, I see my father looking more and more like my Grandpa Frank. I guess that is all part of the cycle of life.

"Your mother told me to drive by after I went to the florist. She knows how much you like your grandparents' house."

"And Grandpa's grapevine." I gave him a hug and a kiss.

"You made good time on the road. I hope you didn't speed."

"Hmmm, if I was, I know where I learned it from." My father loves to drive fast, and so do I. Of course, in Southington, it really doesn't matter how fast you're going. The police tend to pull anyone over who isn't related to an officer. I guess in some ways the town is still small town America.

"I'm glad you're here. Now I won't be the only person your Aunts can talk about. They keep asking your mother when you would be arriving."

My Aunts. I forgot about them. Anyone who comes from an Italian family can appreciate the secret fear I have of my Aunts. Although I have many Aunts, there are only three that cause my blood to boil as I bite my tongue and smile at their prodding questions. They live for weddings and funerals. It is their only time to check out the nieces and nephews who have moved far away. They always travel in a pack, and each seems to have a different job during the interrogation process. First, there is Aunt Sophia, the oldest sister in the pack. Her job is to start up a conversation with the niece or nephew whom the interrogation will be brought upon. Then, there is Aunt Caterina. Her job is to wait and listen for just the right time in the conversation to interrupt with a very personal and intrusive question. And then, there is Aunt Rosetta. Her job may be the most difficult of all. She must remember the responses of all those they interrogate. Then, the aunts visit other friends and families throughout the town and deliver the ever important and necessary news. The other sister of course

5

is my Grandma Marie. I love my Grandma dearly, but she does love to gossip with her sisters. I must say she does protect me when she sees the Aunts making their interrogation triangle toward me. Through the years, I have learned to laugh at their questions and see a little of their thoughtfulness through their interrogations. Now, it will be a little different without Grandpa Frank to hide me from those pesky Aunts, under his grapevine.

"I see you bought a Buick," said my Dad.

"Yes, I knew you would be happy to see me arrive in an American car."

"I guess this book writing thing pays pretty well," he said while opening my car door.

"Yes, things are going very well." My dad still can't comprehend that my job is actually paying the bills. I guess he comes from a generation where a job meant working at a company or factory from nine to five and retiring after twenty-five years with a gold watch. I'm sure, in his eyes, I'm that twelve-year-old girl who received three dollars a week for allowance and spent it on candy and arcade games. He is always asking if I have enough money for food and am I paying my bills on time. I really don't mind his worrying questions. I guess there is a part in all of us that would like to stay twelve years old forever and let someone else do the worrying.

"Dad, I'm sorry I didn't get here sooner." I tried to hold back the tears.

"Don't give it a second thought. You were always there for your Grandpa Frank while he was alive. Always spending summer days with him and listening to all his stories; that seemed to get better with time."

"Those stories he told would make a great book someday."

"Never mind. Let's keep some things in the family."

"Getting nervous," I laughed. "Maybe I shouldn't go see my aunts. Now there are some interesting ladies."

"What's so interesting about your Aunts?" "They are just like anybody else's aunts."

"Oh dad, you have got to get out of Southington more often."

"Just be respectful when we go over your Aunt Sophia's house."

"Deal, when will that be?"

"No time like the present. Follow my car. "

"Do you think I forgot the way to my own Aunt's house?"

"Nope, just want to make sure you don't take a detour. By the way, are you married yet?" shouted my father with a grin.

"Here we go again," I whispered to myself, as I started my American car.

The drive to Aunt Sophia's house involved a right turn at the first stop sign, passed St. Thomas Church, and a quick left onto Pine Road. My Aunt Sophia's house was made of brick. She and her late husband, Geno, would always wash the house every spring and fall. There would always be tons of flowers in their yard and the grass was always cut to perfection. Of course, no one was allowed to walk on the grass. Uncle Geno had laid out perfectly marked paths so one could walk from one side of the yard to the next, without disturbing a blade of grass. Now, the yard is just grass. Aunt Sophia is unable to plant all those flowers anymore and she hires someone to cut the grass. She refuses to hire anyone to help clean the inside of the house. Aunt Sophia and her sisters help clean their homes together. Not only is this a nice sisterly thing to do, but it also gives them the chance to correlate all the gossip they have heard around the town. Then, they can properly share with the ladies at the beauty parlor on Fridays.

"Maggie, your daughter is here," my dad announced as we entered Aunt Sophia's house.

"Oh good, I was worried with all that traffic. Are you hungry? Did you stop for lunch on the way here? We have plenty of food. Sit down and I'll get you a plate. How about something to drink? Vinny, get her some ginger ale. After that long drive, ginger ale is best."

My dad just gave me a wink as he went into the pantry to get the ginger ale. I have yet to give a response to all my mother's questions and yet she already knows the answers. I often wonder why mothers ask their children questions if they are only looking for one particular answer.

"So where is everybody?" I asked my mother.

"They are in the parlor going over the arrangements with the funeral director. Your Grandma wants to keep things simple, but you know your Aunts."

I smiled at my mother as she sat down next to me. My mother is French, not a bit of Italian in her, but she is the world's greatest cook. And that is why, as my dad says, he married her even though she is not Italian. My mom is happiest when she makes other people happy; that usually involves making them food. So, I ate everything on my plate and waited patiently for the Aunts to make their way into the kitchen. As the funeral director walked out the front door with my dad, I knew it wouldn't be much longer.

"Margaret.... has Elizabeth arrived?" I could hear my three Aunts shuffling their feet towards the kitchen. I took a deep breath and mentally prepared myself for the interrogation.

"Yes, she is in the kitchen. I made her a plate with some of the food that was sent over. I hope you don't mind?"

"Mind....oh please, it will just go to waste. Oh my, there she is....Little Elizabeth. I hear you like living in the city and the job is good, yes?" asked Aunt Sophia.

"Oh yes, I like it very much."

"And what is the city like now?" asked my Aunt Caterina. "I remember when I was a young girl."

"When you were a young girl it was safe to walk in Brooklyn at two in the morning. But then again, a proper young lady wouldn't be out walking at two in the morning. You don't go out walking at two in the morning, do you Elizabeth?" asked my Aunt Rosetta.

"Oh no," I responded quickly, and looked towards the parlor for my Grandma Marie.

"Why don't you go keep your Grandma company. Your Aunts and I will prepare all this food for dinner," my mother interrupted.

"Are we having lots of people tonight?" asked Aunt Sophia.

"Oh yes, many nieces and nephews are staying at hotels. I thought it would be nice to have everybody eat a good meal before the two long days ahead."

"That is a wonderful idea Maggie," smiled Aunt Sophia, as she looked at her two sisters.

"Sounds like you better get a pad and pencil to take notes," I said quietly, walking into the parlor.

I entered the parlor and saw my Grandma Marie sitting in a chair. She was looking at a wall where all the wedding pictures of family are on display.

"Searching for mine?" I walked over and gave my grandma a hug.

"You look good Elizabeth. Did you get something to eat?"

"Yes Grandma, I did. How are you doing?"

"Between you and me Elizabeth, I miss your Grandfather and there is a place in my heart that yearns for him to come back to me. But I also feel so blessed to have known and loved such a man. Someday, I hope you will know such a love." She took my hand and gazed back at the wall.

"I heard Aunt Sophia is saving me a spot on that wall."

"Ahhh, your Aunt Sophia."

"She's your sister."

"And she means well. You be nice to your Aunts, no matter how crazy they are. You promise to tell me when I get crazy?"

"Absolutely." I took my Grandma Marie's hand and walked into the kitchen.

"Marie, can I get you some food?" asked Aunt Sophia.

I always find it amusing how my Aunts try to solve every life obstacle with food. I guess it comes from a time when they remember not having a bounty of food. I walked my Grandma Marie to the kitchen table and we sat down. The table was covered with every type of food that either reheats beautifully, freezes beautifully, or just requires little fuss to be presented beautifully at the table. Your typical pre-wake, post-wake, prefuneral, and post-funeral food.

I really wasn't thinking too much about the food. My eyes caught a glimpse of Grandpa Frank's cigar box set on the corner table of Aunt Sophia's kitchen. My Grandpa Frank had a cigar box at all the Aunts' homes. He always kept it well supplied. He had cigar boxes at a few other homes too, including my folks' house. My mind started to drift back to one of my first memories of the cigar box Grandpa Frank kept at my childhood home.

"Take it, it's just one. Don't be a weenie."

"I'm not a weenie and I will take one. But not to prove I'm not a weenie to you Johnny. I'm taking one because I want to take one, so there."

"Stop your girlie explaining and just take one before Grandpa Frank comes back from his walk."

"How's this one look?" I asked my cousin Johnny, the twelve-year-old connoisseur of cigars.

"Oh, they all look the same. Come on, let's go."

I ran as fast as my Ked sneakers would let me and followed Johnny behind my folks' garage. I was eleven years old and, as my mother would say, the most curious child she ever set her eyes upon. My curiosity would find me on this spring day of 1982 behind my folks' garage attempting to smoke my first cigar. I had mentioned my curiosity of what a cigar tastes like to Johnny. Being ever the gentleman, he took it upon himself to help me find out.

"Did you bring any matches?" asked Johnny.

"Matches? I'm not allowed to use matches."

"Oh my God, I'm dealing with an amateur here."

"Oh, like you're so cool."

"Cool enough to know we need freaking matches to smoke cigars. I'll be right back."

I waited patiently with Grandpa Frank's cigar in my hand. I brought the cigar to my nose, just like Grandpa Frank does before he lights it. It didn't smell that bad. I put the cigar in my mouth and practiced taking puffs and holding it properly. I heard the crack of a twig and peeked around the corner of the garage. I went to look up, but a pair of black pants stopped my nose. They weren't Johnny's. I could recognize those black pants anywhere. They were my Grandpa Frank's. My Grandpa Frank always wore black pants and a crisp white shirt. He even mowed the lawn in black pants and a white shirt. Once I asked him why he didn't have another color of pants to wear. He

10

laughed and said he would go shopping for a new pair of pants when these wore out.

"Hello Elizabeth Marie Manciano," Grandpa Frank said with a smile.

Ahh, the usage of one's full name. That's when every kid knows they are in some serious crapola. "Hello Grandpa Frank. How are you on this beautiful spring day?"

"It is a beautiful spring day. I love this time of year. One can smell the earth starting to wake all the flowers from their winter rest. Would you like to walk with me Elizabeth?"

"Sure. Where are we going?" I hopped up from the ground and secretly tucked the cigar into the back pocket of my Levi's.

"I have to stop at Mr. Ferrucci's to sharpen my pruning blades. It's time to clean up the grape vine again."

I loved walking with my Grandpa Frank and I especially liked walking to Mr. Ferrucci's. He always had a jar of candy at his hardware store and he always let me have two pieces. One for each dimple, he would say.

"Hello Mr. Ferrucci," shouted my Grandpa Frank as we walked into the store.

"Bonjourna." Mr. Ferrucci came from the back room with two glasses of wine. "Let's make a toast to another good year for Frankie's grapes."

"Sounds good to me."

"And how is Elizabeth today?" asked Mr. Ferrucci. "Have you been a good girl?"

"I don't know." I shyly looked at my Grandpa Frank. "I haven't done anything wrong yet today."

"Well, that's good enough for me. Tell me, do you still have your dimples?"

"Yes." I gave him a huge smile.

"Ah yes, I see them clear as day. I guess that means you may take two pieces of candy."

"Thank you, Mr. Ferrucci." I ran to the candy jar near the cash register.

"Just eat one now Elizabeth. You may need the other one later."

"Okay Grandpa Frank."

"You know Frank, I have some new pruning shears. Very well made. Let me show you."

"I like the ones I have, thank you. These shears are the only shears that have touched my grape vine on Goat's Island."

"Your Grandpa is a stubborn man Elizabeth. Doesn't want to change with the times."

"I'll change with the times when the change is an improvement. Come on Elizabeth. Let's see what Grandma has made for lunch."

"I hope it's pasta fagoli. Grandma makes the best pasta fagoli, right Grandpa Frank?"

"Absolutely. Only because she is the best cook in the whole world."

"Grandpa, what were you like as a little boy?"

"Oh, I got into a little mischief now and then."

"What's mischief?"

"Mischief is what you were getting into with your cousin Johnny behind the garage. Why don't you share what you have in your pocket."

"I just wanted to see what it tastes like. And Johnny said it would make me feel like a grown up." I shyly handed the cigar to my Grandpa Frank.

"I see. Well, I feel like a grown up every day and sometimes I wish I could feel like a kid."

"You're not going to tell on me are you Grandpa Frank?"

"Hmmm, let's see. I'll give you a test to figure out how grown up you really are. And if you pass, maybe then I'll have to call you Miss Elizabeth. Does that sound more grown up to you?"

"Oh yes. You know, I am eleven and I'm getting a ten-speed bike next week."

"Well then, let's take the test. Give me what is in your other pocket."

"Huh? You want my candy?"

"Don't you want to be a grown up?"

"Okay." I hesitantly handed him the second piece of candy.

"Now then, I have one item in each of my hands. First, I have a cigar in my right hand. Next, I have a piece of candy in my left hand. Elizabeth, which item do you really want to have?" Grandpa Frank had the look of a scholar.

"Well, I guess, when it comes right down to it.....there really is nothing better than Mr. Ferrucci's candy." I grabbed the piece of candy from my Grandpa's hand and popped it into my mouth.

"Well then, since you passed the test, I guess you have officially become Miss Elizabeth." Grandpa Frank smiled as he kissed me on the cheek.

"I did? You mean I really am a grown up?" I hugged him excitedly.

"Yes Miss Elizabeth, you are exactly where you are supposed to be."

"Elizabeth, honey, are you with us dear?" asked my mother, as she rubbed my back.

"Oh yes, my mind just wandered for a minute." I looked around the room a bit puzzled, as I sat at my Aunt Sophia's kitchen table.

"Would you like daddy to bring you home and you can rest for a while? I have your old bedroom all fixed up for you. You can come back in a few hours. Then all your cousins will be here."

"That sounds like a good idea." I kissed my mother and reached for my coat.

The Old Neighborhood

My dad pulled out of Pine Road and passed St. Thomas Church. In a few days, we would all be at the church saying goodbye to Grandpa Frank.

"Would you like me to drive thru downtown before I take you back to the house?"

"Sure, but from what I saw, a lot of downtown isn't what I remember."

"Yes, the invasion of the all about me," laughed my father.

My father used this saying when referring to people who want it all and don't care who they step on to get there. They are the people, in his eyes, who ruined his once upon a time-small and quaint American town. They work in the city, but want to live in the country. They still want all the quick conveniences of the city, so they replace the farms with malls. They turn the other way when family businesses are forced to close. They build extravagant homes and then complain about the taxes. They rent fancy cars, and claim them as business expenses. They place their kids in day care, because they need the two incomes. Then, they grumble at the end of the day, because of no quality time with their family.

"Seems to me, we had less in my day, but we were a lot happier."

"Maybe that is how some people want to live," I said to my father.

"Running here and there, having somebody else raise your kids, living in a home with more rooms than you have people to put in them. Sorry, that's not how I raised my kids."

"I know, I'm just saying."

"A Starbucks right downtown here. People spend four to five dollars a day on a styrofoam cup filled with some coffee. In my day, you could buy a bag of groceries with four or five dollars."

We passed Main Street and the Town Green. Same old gazebo was there with the old timers reflecting on better days. My Grandpa Frank never sat at the gazebo with the other old men. He always said people spend too much time talking about the past. When you do that, you waste your today and have no plans for the future. Grandpa Frank was a big believer in leaving things better than the way you found them. I guess that's why he loved caring for his yard so much. When he and Grandma Marie bought the house, it was neglected. My dad said he can remember his father coming home from work and removing tree stumps from the back yard. Grandpa Frank would say, 'Vincent, someday we will have the world's best grapevine right here in our very own backyard.' He saw things the way they could be. I think he instilled that vision in me.

As we turned onto my old street of Green Hill Drive, my eyes glanced at the familiar homes. They were once filled with neighborhood friends and adoptive parents and grandparents. There was Mr. & Mrs. Nuccio's home right next to my folks; the oldest married couple known to mankind. Ever since I can recall, Mr. Nuccio has been retired. He spends his time doing yard work and telling the other neighbors how to do their yard work. Across from my folks lived a widowed Irish lady, Mrs. Shea. She would watch my sister and I play from her window when I was younger. Sometimes I would sit on her porch with her on summer days. She always had cool stories to tell about life in the old days. Next to the widow Shea was a two family house. It was owned by the D'Agostino's. They lived on the first floor with their children. There was always a family moving in or out on the second floor. This provided my sister and me with new kids to play with after school on a rotating basis. The Copeland's lived next to the D'Agostino's in the biggest house on Green Hill Drive. Mr. Copeland owned a few factories in town and had lots of money. They never had any kids, so they adopted the kids in the neighborhood. Their backyard had an awesome hill for sledding, and they would open their backyard to all the kids after a snowfall. Across the street from the Copeland's lived another couple with a few kids of their own, the Napolitano's. Their daughter would play Barbie's with my sister. I preferred to climb the ancient maple tree in their backyard with their son, Matthew. My cousin Johnny would climb with us, too. We would dare each other to climb higher. There was a perfect spot just about halfway to the top that I'd like to sit and check out the view. You could see all of downtown Southington from that particular spot; even the lumberyard my dad owned. Sometimes, I could see him loading the trucks and talking to the other merchants that worked downtown. If I climbed that tree today, all those stores have disappeared.

"We're home," said my dad as he opened the car door for me.

"Sorry, I was daydreaming about the old neighborhood."

"Nothing old about this neighborhood except the tenants."

As I walked to the back door, I looked over at the Napolitano's house. The maple tree was still standing, but the swing-set and pool were replaced with a patio and flower garden. The sliding door opened and I saw an older lady start walking outside.

"Mrs. Napolitano?" I shouted over the shrubs.

"Elizabeth...is that you? My, you've become a lady."

"Hi. So you're still living here, huh?"

"Oh yes. You know, when you find great neighbors, why move."

"These kids don't know what it's like to stay in one place very long. They are always looking for something better. The secret to finding perfection is taking what you have and making it work." My father always enjoyed these mini lectures.

"How do you like New York?" asked Mrs. Napolitano.

"I like it very much thanks. Always something to do."

"Your Grandpa always bragged about you whenever we saw him in the stores or on his walks. I will miss seeing him around town."

"He lived a long life and he enjoyed every bit of it."

"You're right, Vincent. Mr. Napolitano and I will be at the wake and the church services. Marie is such a good person. Tell her she is in our thoughts and prayers."

"Will do," said my dad as he unlocked the back door.

I started to walk up the steps. I turned and looked across the street to Mrs. Shea's home. I looked at her picture window. The drapes that once hung there in my youth have since been replaced with blinds by the new owner. I recalled running home from grammar school every day and always waving to Mrs. Shea. She would always watch out her window to make sure I arrived home safely from school. I never thought much of it until the day Mrs. Shea was taking away by an ambulance. I was twelve years old .....

"Mom, what's going on?" I ran up our driveway towards the back steps where my mother was standing.

"Relax, Mrs. Shea must have fallen or something. They will take her to the hospital. She will be just fine."

The emergency personnel carefully place Mrs. Shea into the ambulance. She looked so tiny lying on the stretcher. I couldn't believe what my eyes were seeing. Just yesterday, I was talking to her on her porch. I promised to weed her flower garden this Saturday. She was going to pay me two dollars. I just couldn't sit on the stoop and watch what was happening. I needed someone to tell me everything was going to be all right.

"Mom, I'm taking my bike to Grandpa Frank's. I'll call you when I get there."

"Okay, Elizabeth. Watch yourself when you cross the streets."

I hopped on my Huffy ten-speed bike and cruised down Green Hill Drive. I passed my hometown bank, crossed the street at the market and turned left at the tracks and entered Goat's Island. I turned into my grandparents' driveway.

"Grandma," I shouted through the screen door. "Can you call my mom and tell her I'm here?"

"Sure Little Elizabeth, your Grandpa is out back tending to his grapevine. I'll be right out with some juice and cookies."

"Grandpa," I shouted as I ran to the backyard.

"Miss Elizabeth....what's wrong child?" He scooped me up in his arms.

"Oh Grandpa, it's just terrible...everything is just terrible."

"Nothing can be so terrible to make a pretty girl cry. Come, sit with your Grandpa Frank under the grapevine. Let's hear about this terrible you talk about."

"It's Mrs. Shea," I said while trying to catch my breath. "She was taken away in an ambulance. I was walking home from school and saw everything. Mommy said everything would be all right, but she doesn't know anything. What if I never see her again?"

"Hmmm, that is a terrible thing to see. You saw a good friend hurt and there is nothing you can do to make her better again. Yes, you have a good reason to cry Miss Elizabeth." He wiped away my tears with his handkerchief.

"How about some juice and cookies to help dry up those tears?" Grandma Marie walked towards the grapevine with a tray.

"Our Miss Elizabeth comes with some sad news about Mrs. Shea. She was taken away in an ambulance today."

"Yes, your mother told me all about it on the phone. She was going to call Mr. Shea's son after dinner to see what happened. Maybe we can go to the hospital tomorrow after your school day?"

"They won't let kids in those places. You have to be really old to see anybody."

I took another bite from my oatmeal cookie.

"Well, don't you worry about that. You be ready for us after school tomorrow. Your Grandma and I will take you to the hospital to visit our friend Mrs. Shea."

"Really, Grandpa Frank?"

"Really. I would never lie to a pretty girl. Isn't that right Marie?"

"Absolutely true." She took my Grandpa's hand and kissed him on the cheek. "Are you staying for dinner?"

"I can't tonight. It's shells and meatballs at my house tonight. My favorite."

"Well then, you best be getting home. And don't forget about tomorrow."

"I won't." I gave my grandparents a hug.

"Frank, give the child some money for candy. She can stop for something sweet on the way home."

"Yes Marie." Grandpa Frank jingled the coins in his pocket. "Tell me Miss Elizabeth, what is the candy of the week?"

"I really like Three Musketeers this week."

"All right. This should be enough for one candy Three Musketeer bar." He plopped the coins in the palm of my hand.

"Thanks Grandpa Frank. I'll see you tomorrow."

The school bell finally rang...3:15. Another wasted day in the sixth grade. I ran out the school doors with my Pac-Man backpack swinging in the air. I crossed the street and ran to the corner. My father's lumberyard was located right at the corner, before I turned up the big hill of Green Hill Drive. Grandpa Frank and Grandma Marie were waiting at my daddy's office. I ran into the office and kissed my dad.

"So, how was your day at school Elizabeth?"

"Boring." I tossed my backpack on a chair.

"How can school be so boring?" asked my Grandpa Frank. "There is so much to learn. In America, you can learn about anything you want."

"No you can't Grandpa Frank. The teacher decides what you're going to learn. They only teach what's in the teacher's books, because all the answers are in there for them."

"Watch your tone." My father squished my face. "Your teacher has to put up with you all day."

"Not funny." I started to walk over to the Pong arcade game.

"Don't get started with that game. Your grandparents are taking you to see Mrs. Shea now."

"Agh, those silly games," said my Grandma Marie, "I hope they're just a fad."

"I think so," said my father. "Who would want to spend all that money on a game? One of the merchants loaned me this one. I think he's hoping the guys will want to buy one for their kids at Christmas."

"Are people buying them?"

"Yes, Dad. But I don't know about all this Atari stuff."

"This generation seems to spend money on anything that makes them happy. What did someone call for yesterday, Marie?"

"A.....American Express."

"Oh yes, American Express. Maybe you can buy everything in America with this American Express. I told the lady on the phone I have everything I need. If I may need something new, I can find it at Mr.Ferrucci's store. Where I pay cash. Yes, Elizabeth?"

"Yes, I like Mr. Ferrucci. He has good candy."

"Speaking of candy." Grandpa Frank started to pull some candy out of his pocket.

"Now Dad, the girl gets enough candy."

"Well then, we can all share the candy while we walk to the hospital....yes?"

"Why don't you take the car?"

"Because I have strong, healthy legs Vincent. And my legs don't cost me 73 cents a gallon."

"Can you believe the price of gasoline?" asked my Grandma Marie.

"It's not that bad."

"Don't say that Vincent. Don't buy the gas. You kids keep buying the gas and they will keep moving up the prices. You mark my words."

"I think we better start walking," interrupted my Grandma Marie. "We want to have Elizabeth home for dinner time."

I walked up to the nurses' station with my Grandpa Frank and waited by his side.

"I'm sorry Frank, but children are not allowed to visit the patients."

"I see." Grandpa Frank scratched the side of his face and flattened his mustache. "How are the grapes I gave your husband, Joseph, last summer? Did they make a fine wine?"

"Now, I wouldn't know about that. I just made some delicious jam."

"Well then, I can teach Joseph how to make some wine in the fall. Give you some time with him out of your hair, as you ladies like to say."

"Time alone. I wouldn't know what to do with myself. It does sound nice."

"You are a lady of beauty and wisdom." Grandpa Frank kissed the nurse's hand.

I giggled as my Grandpa Frank took my hand. We went all the way to the top floor, number four. We stepped out of the elevator and everything was quiet. I saw nurses behind a tall desk. I peeked in the rooms, as we walked down the hallway. I saw mostly old people lying in beds and machines beeping. I wondered if Mrs. Shea would have a machine beeping in her room, too.

Grandpa Frank quietly knocked on the door and waited for a response.

"Come in." Mrs. Shea sounded like we had woken her up from a nap.

"Well, don't you look lovely today," Grandpa Frank said.

"Oh, your eyesight must be going," laughed Mrs. Shea.

I smiled and was a bit relieved that Mrs. Shea still had her sense of humor.

"How are you doing? I saw the ambulance take you away yesterday when I was coming home from school."

"Yes, I remember waiting for you by my window. The room started to spin a bit. Luckily, my daughter-in-law makes me wear this little necklace that calls the police if I get hurt. The next thing I remember is being at the hospital. Everyone was very excited, running every which way. Oh, they were giving me a headache."

"I'll never figure out how people are supposed to rest in hospitals when people keep poking you. And all the noise," interrupted my Grandma Marie.

"Are you coming home soon?" I asked Mrs. Shea.

Everyone smiled. Mrs. Shea turned and looked out the window for a few moments.

"I don't think I'll be returning to Green Hill Drive, Elizabeth. You see, when people get older, their bodies don't get better as fast as when you're young. I need to go to another place to help my bones get healthy."

"After that, then you can come home?"

"Oh the youth, so eager for answers," laughed my Grandma Marie. "I think we better let Mrs. Shea rest. We can visit tomorrow. Yes Frank?"

"Yes, Marie, that is a good idea."

I walked over to Mrs. Shea and kissed her on the cheek. I told her I would see her tomorrow after school. I promised to bring my creative writing journal and read her one of my stories. Mrs. Shea always liked listening to the stories I wrote in Mrs. Kalosky's creative writing class. It was the only cool thing about going to school for me that year. It was the only subject I did well in.

"Are you coming Elizabeth?" asked my father.

"What? Yes. I was just thinking about when Mrs. Shea was taken away in the ambulance."

"That was a hard year for everybody. She was the first person to leave the neighborhood. I think the first funeral you went to, right?"

"Yeah. I still don't like wakes."

"Are you going to be okay at the services?"

"I'll just keep thinking that Grandpa Frank can now visit Mrs. Shea. He can tell her the stories I made her listen to are in books now."

"I don't think you made her listen to anything. She really enjoyed your company."

"How did she die? Really?"

"Your mother and I told you the truth. Her heart just stopped. Grandpa Frank always said she died the best way possible."

"What did he mean by that? Sounds a little morbid to me."

"I guess he meant she died with dignity. She got to live in her house and wasn't hooked up to machines. She left everyone with happy memories of a vibrant and interesting lady."

"Just like Grandpa Frank. I never got a chance to say goodbye to both of them. I must be cursed."

"I think it's more important that you always said hello."

My father. Sometimes I don't think he realizes how much he says.

I walked into my childhood home. I was anxious to take off my coat, shoes and relax. My father went to his office to make some phone calls. I took my suitcase upstairs to my old room. As I walked up the stairs, I gazed at all the old family pictures hung on the wall. There were pictures of me when I was a little kid. Pictures of my grandfather when he was a little kid. I always loved the old family portraits of my great-grandparents surrounded by their children. Everyone looked so formal and stern. It is hard to tell if they were happy. My father would always say people didn't worry about all the little things that we do now. People accepted what they had and lived the best way they could. I don't think I would have liked to have lived back then. I like being a free spirit and trying new things. That wasn't too popular of a lifestyle for woman back then. I walked into my old bedroom and crashed on the bed. The furniture was pretty much the same. My track trophies and smurf collection have been packed away. It's funny how the things we treasure so much as a child become things revisited as an adult with just a smile. There is one trophy I keep at my office. It reminds me of what is really of value in this world. Lying on my bed, I begin to think of the day I earned that trophy. My Grandpa Frank was there to wipe my tears.

"Come on ladies, they are going to start in one minute." My track coach shouted to me and my best friend, Katy. Katy and I had been best friends since grade two. We shared a midnight blue crayon together while making Halloween posters. Now, we were juniors in High School and on the track team. I loved running. Katy was pretty good at it too. Unfortunately, she wasn't as good as her father would have liked. That bothered her. Grandpa Frank was always there to cheer Katy and me. He always said it's good for him to be around young people. It keeps his mind off dying.

"Grandpa Frank. I got a problem."

"Are you hurt, Elizabeth?"

"No, No...it's nothing like that. This is our last meet for the year. Katy hasn't won any events this spring. I think we are the top two compared to all the other runners here. If it's just her and me at the end, maybe I should slow down a little?"

"Hmmm, that could be a problem, but not for me."

"Oh great, I knew you would have an answer."

"Just a minute. I said that wouldn't be a problem for me. I know what I would do, but what would you do?"

"I don't think you understand my situation here Grand-"

"Yes, I do. Now you have to ask yourself, what will you do? What do you value? What do you hope someone would do for you?"

"This shits."

"Heh, all that money on a Catholic education and this is the only word you can speak?"

"Sorry Grandpa."

"Go. You go run now. Your coach is having an attack with his heart."

"It's called a heart attack, Grandpa Frank."

"So, it is. Yes....go-go-go!"

I took my place for the fifty-yard dash. I glanced over at Katy. She looked really nervous and just kept her head down. The gun sounded and we were off. Katy and I were quickly in the lead. As we approached the finish line, I slowed my pace. Katy crossed the line first. She had won the trophy for our final event.

About ten years later, I received a package in the mail. I thought it was a package of cookies from my mother. She would always send me cookies when I was feeling sad. About a week earlier, I told my parents I wouldn't be coming home for the Apple Harvest Festival. My book had been rejected for the 100th time. I started to believe I would be stuck in my editing job forever. I got a glass of chocolate milk and sat down at the table with my box. I looked at the return address, but didn't recognize the last name. I opened the box and saw a trophy. It was the trophy Katy had won that day in the spring of our junior year. Under the trophy was a letter.

Dear Elizabeth,
I saw your folks at the Apple Harvest last weekend. They told me about all your exciting endeavors. I can remember when we talked about living in Manhattan together and writing the world's greatest novel. You always knew exactly what you wanted to do, and you never let fear get in the way. I always admired you for that (and maybe was a little bit jealous at times too!). Looking back at our friendship, I feel like I owe you one. I guess that's why I'm writing this letter. When you gave me the race that junior year (and don't lie and tell me you didn't), it showed you valued our friendship more than winning a race or a trophy. Through the years, certain things would happen and I would recall that feeling of having a friend in my life that would make such a sacrifice, just to make me happy. I can't remember the feeling I had when they put that trophy in my hand. I'll always remember seeing you and your Grandpa Frank smiling and cheering the loudest when they presented me the trophy.

Anyway, the attached business card is a publishing company in Georgia. I'm sure they will read your book and give you an honest review. It's sad that the business has turned into creating best sellers, instead of writing best sellers. However, I am certain that quality will always prevail, and you Elizabeth have a lot of quality. Good luck. Let me know when you meet with the chief editor. I'll have him drive you to my home for dinner. Don't worry; he is a very well-mannered guy. After all, I married him!
Love & Friendship, Katy #12 ☺

I did travel to Georgia and had my manuscript read by Katy's very well- mannered husband. My book was published the following year. Unfortunately, I had to come to the realization that writing is like any other business. Sometimes it's connections and not just quality that opens doors. However, it's always comforting to work with people that you trust and have your best interest at heart. My Grandpa Frank always said you attract who you are. Sometimes people come into our lives to remind us of who we are not supposed to be. Our true courage is revealed when we do not falter to their evil ways. 'It takes a lot of courage to accept who you are and what you believe in. It takes even greater courage when you remain true to yourself, when surrounded by those who do not share your values. That is a person I hope to always be. The only type of person I would call a friend.' That's what my Grandpa Frank would say. Some people might say I got lucky. A fortunate coincidence that Katy decided to attend the Apple Harvest. I say it has nothing to do with luck. It's constant preparation. Ready when the opportunity comes in fulfilling your dreams. Maybe it is a little fun to believe in that fate stuff, too. Then again, I was never into being saved by the handsome knight. I was fortunate enough to have my Grandpa Frank around while growing up. He taught me to drive a car. Just in case my handsome knight never arrived, I could drive myself to the ball.

I opened my eyes in my old bedroom and looked at the clock. It was five o'clock. I walked down the hallway to my parents' bedroom. My Dad was lying in bed watching the news.

"Hey, sleepy head."

"Hey back at you. I'm gonna take a shower. Then maybe we can go back to Aunt Sophia's place. Unfortunately," I tried to whisper without him hearing.

"I heard that. You be nice. Someday you will be old, too."

"Yes. I can live with getting old, but I know I won't be a nosy pest."

"You forget. If your Aunt Sophia wasn't so nosy, Grandpa Frank and you might still be in the Montague's pond."

"Oh yeah. I almost forgot about that day."

"Convincing Grandpa Frank to teach you how to drive at fourteen years old. A very short fourteen too, I might add."

"No need to remind me. I remember quite well how short I was. Just to set the record straight, Grandpa Frank offered to teach me. I remember it all so well."

"Now Elizabeth, just remember to not step on the accelerator all at once. You want to start slowly." Grandpa Frank instructed, as I sat behind the wheel of his Buick Skylark.

"I think I've got it. Can I try to go forward now?"

"Okay, let's give it a chance."

"It's give it a try, Grandpa."

"Yes, yes...whatever you young kids say."

"Now watch the tree. Try to turn into Mr. Montague's driveway. We can turn around in his yard. He has that big backyard. All French people have big yards, because all those children. They need a place to run around. It is true Miss Elizabeth. Those Frenchies are wild people."

"Hey, remember my mother is French."

"Oh yes well...ummmm....of course it helps when these wild Frenchies marry us good-looking Italians."

"Okay, I'll forgive you."

"Elizabeth. Watch the dip in the back here."

Crash!! The car was suddenly sinking into this dip in Mr. Montague's backyard. Aunt Sophia, whose backyard was adjacent to Mr. Montague's, came running out from her porch door.

"Oh Mother of Jesus! Mother of Jesus! Please save us!" Aunt Sophia screamed as she ran towards the Buick.

"Calm down Sophia." Grandpa Frank leaned out the passenger window. "Instead of bothering the Virgin Mary all the time, how about knocking on Mr. Montague's door and getting us some help."

It wasn't long before Mr. Montague came running out the door.

"Good afternoon to you. Sorry about driving into this little dip here."

"Dip." laughed Mr. Montague. "Frank, this is the beginning of a hole for my pool."

"A pool? Why do you want a pool in your backyard? There's a free one at the town park."

"It's the newest thing. And pretty soon everybody will have a pool. Just like they do in those rich neighborhoods in California."

"Well now, isn't that something. People wasting their money on something they can already get for free. I use the pool at the park...with all the other hard-working, tax-paying Americans. I am American citizen now."

"Oh, would you two stop carrying on and get this car out of the mud. You have a little girl in there."

"I'm not so little, Aunt Sophia. I'm fourteen."

"You're not scared, are you Elizabeth?" asked my Grandpa Frank.

"No."

"I wouldn't worry about Elizabeth," screeched Aunt Sophia. "What do you plan on telling Marie?"

"And I suppose you will offer to tell her if I don't? Don't worry Elizabeth. It wasn't your fault we landed in this dippy pool thing of Mr. Montague's. It's his fault. Putting a hole in such a ridiculous spot. These French people have no smarts when planning how to do things. That's why they never won a war on their own."

"I suppose Aunt Sophia saved us that day. I'll never forget my first driving lesson."

"Good, now take a shower. Your mother called before. She said to wear something comfortable and warm. It's the fall, and the nights get cool in the country."

"Really. It gets cool at night in the city, too!"

All cleaned up and waiting for my father, I decided to sit on the back steps and take in some crisp New England Fall air. Mrs. Napolitano walked over carrying a plate of food.

"I know you probably already have a lot of food at your Grandma's house. This plate of cookies is just for you Elizabeth."

"Not your famous gingerbread man cookies?"

"I remember how you, Johnny and my Matthew used to eat the whole plate of them. Especially after sledding all day at the Copeland's."

"Now there's a flashback. Those were some of the best no school snow days I ever had."

"And one day it was the best school day- snow day you three ever had. Do you remember that day?"

"You are such a baby....baby, baby, baby!" Johnny and I screamed at Matthew as he started to walk to school.

"I just don't want to spend all day outside. Where are we supposed to go when it gets cold? Huh? Tell me that fart heads."

Johnny and I thought for a moment. I yelled to Matthew to wait up. I had an idea. We ran to the Copeland's shed and dropped off our backpacks and lunchboxes. We waited until all the other kids walking to grammar school had passed our neighborhood.

"Yippee," screamed Matthew as he went sliding down Copeland's Hill.

"Not so loud," said Johnny. "We don't want Mrs. Copeland to hear us."

"They already left for their Christmas trip to Pennsylvania." I grabbed my sled and sat down at the top of the hill.

Everybody was having a great time. The morning seemed to go by much faster than when we were at school. Around noon, we decided to eat lunch.

"I'm getting cold out here," Matthew said, with a mouthful of peanut butter and fluff. "Let's go into Mr. & Mrs. Copeland's house just for a little bit."

"We can't. That's like a crime. The police will come with guns and handcuffs and take us away. Besides, remember my plan?" I asked Matthew.

"Oh yeah, the fire."

"Fire? What's this about a freaking fire?"

"Relax Johnny. We'll just make a small one in the shed to get warm. Then we'll put it out."

"Okay smarty pants. How do you plan on starting the fire? We don't have any matches."

"No problem." I walked towards an old corner cabinet in the shed and opened a drawer. "Look at this."

"It's one of your Grandpa Frank's cigar boxes. How did you know it was there?" asked Matthew.

"I saw my Grandpa Frank and Mr. Copeland smoking one day. Mr. Copeland made me promise not to tell his wife. But he never made me promise not to tell you guys." I showed Johnny a box of matches from the cigar box.

"What are we waiting for? Let's get some heat in this place."

We collected some branches and took them back to the shed.

"It's not working," moaned Matthew. "The twigs are too wet from the snow."

"Wait guys. I got an idea." Johnny reached up high on a shelf and grabbed a jar of my Grandpa Frank's homemade wine.

"Wait a minute, Johnny. I heard my Grandpa's wine puts a fire in your stomach without a match. I don't think this is such a good idea."

"Now who's being the baby?"

"Yeah, now who?"

I pushed Matthew down to the floor to shut him up.

"Just get some smoke going. I'll pour a little wine over it and it will be fine. Trust me."

When someone ends a sentence with the words trust me, you should run in the opposite direction as fast as you can. I didn't. Johnny poured my Grandpa Frank's wine over the fire. I don't know what my Grandpa puts in his wine, but I've never saw a fire like that. Flames just danced to the top of the ceiling. An enormous crackling noise was made in that tiny wooden shed. Johnny, being the bravest of us all, was the first one to run out the door. I grabbed Matthew with my right hand and my Mickey Mouse lunch box with the other. We ran right behind Johnny. He ran into Grandpa Frank.

"Is today a holiday? Is today the day when all Italian children don't have to go to school? Hmmm, I didn't hear Mr. Bob Steele mention anything on the radio. A very smart man don't you know. Let's see, I think the word of the day is-"

"Grandpa Frank," I interrupted. You have to do something about the fire."

"Oh, I did. The fire truck should be here any minute. I saw your little smoke. Mr. Copeland asked me to watch the place. He also asked me to see what spot in the yard would be a good place for a grapevine. I guess you found our little supply of wine, yes? Why didn't you just drink the wine to stay warm, instead of starting a fire?"

"We are too young to drink," answered Matthew.

"Oh, I see. Playing with fire...this is okay? You destroyed a man's property, but it will all be fixed."

Are you going to have it fixed before Mr. & Mrs. Copeland come home?"

"No Elizabeth. You children will rebuild the shed this spring."

"But we don't know how to build stuff."

"Well then Johnny, maybe you should go to school. I heard it's a place where they teach you all kinds of things."

"I'm glad we all gave you guys a laugh." My father joined Mrs. Napolitano and me at the back steps.

"I was ready to ground you for life. Your Grandpa said the child will learn nothing just sitting in her room. No, he had a better idea."

"Making us work our entire spring vacation to rebuild that shed. I think I still have the blisters."

"I remember your Grandpa Frank just sitting in his lawn chair with his cigar. Watching you children work. There were inspections every afternoon, too."

"Yeah, and Grandpa Frank's inspections weren't that easy to pass. We had to leave everything as neat as a pin every day before we went home."

"Well, my Matthew must have remembered that rule. He makes his workers do the same thing at the construction site."

"Matthew is a hard worker," interrupted my dad. "He has a good reputation in town for building fine homes."

"My Matthew loves his work. He has the hammer Frank gave him after rebuilding that shed."

"I remember that. Grandpa Frank gave Johnny, Matthew and me hammers the day we finished the shed. He said now we have a trade and we will never go hungry. We just laughed at the time. Now, a lot of the things he said make more sense."

"That's called getting old," said Mrs. Napolitano with a laugh. "We realize too late how important our elders are. How much we can learn from them."

"I think Elizabeth let her Grandpa Frank know how special he was to her."

"I hope I did, dad. Maybe there is a way I can make sure everyone else learns a little something from him, too."

"Just tell your Aunts what you want the world to know. Consider them the AT&T of the family."

"Thanks for reminding me about them."

"You're welcome. Come on, you can eat those cookies on the way to your Aunt Sophia's."

"Thanks. And thanks Mrs. Napolitano for the gingerbread man cookies."

"You're welcome, Elizabeth. I'll see you at the wake."

My dad and I walked towards the garage. Suddenly, we heard a woman's voice from across the street.

"I need you to do it today," screamed Mrs. D'Agostino to a young man.

"Who is Mrs. D'Agostino screaming at?"

"Her son. Does he look a little different to you?"

"He looks a little scary."

"Well, drugs change people."

"Drugs? Who would have thought the perfect family on the block would have a kid that got into drugs."

"Remember what Grandpa used to say....if things look perfect, you probably had too much wine."

"They did have some tough times. I remember that morning when the police came to their front door...."

"What's all the noise out there," shouted my mother from the screen door.

"Something is going on at the D'Agostino's place. There's a police car. Maybe they're here for their tenants on the second floor." Grandpa Frank loaded all the camping equipment in the car.

My mother opened the screen door and leaned out to shake her dust mop. "The new tenants have been real quiet."

"They don't have any kids and they're really old. Like thirty-five." I answered with a smirk on my almost seventeen year old face.

"I didn't know they were that old, Miss Elizabeth. Where's Johnny? That boy is always late. No responsibility. When I was his age, I had three jobs."

"Don't worry dad," my father interrupted, as he came outside with some duffel bags. "Once those drill sergeants get a hold of him, he'll be a new man."

"Someone mention drill sergeants?" Johnny ran up the driveway with his duffel bag in one hand and a donut in the other.

"You better stop eating that kind of food."

"I got one more month until I leave for basic training Uncle Vincent. I'm going to eat whatever I want. Besides, I'm a senior in high school; I'm supposed to have all the fun I want."

"Something doesn't look right over there." My mother watched the police officers talk to Mr. & Mrs. D'Agostino.

"Here comes Mrs. Napolitano with her son in their car. Maybe they know what's going on. Mrs. Napolitano usually knows everybody's business," I said.

Mrs. Napolitano and her son, Matthew, got out of the car. Her daughter, Laura, ran out the front door and gave her brother a hug. They walked into the house. Mrs. Napolitano walked towards my mother with tears in her eyes.

"Good Morning everybody. I see you're taking the kids on their annual spring time camping trip. I hate to give you such terrible news before you leave. I think the kids would like to know what has happened."

"Please sit down." Grandpa Frank placed a lawn chair beside my mother, who was sitting on the steps.

"Thank you." Mrs. Napolitano took a breath. "I received a call early this morning from Matthew. He was at the hospital with Alison. Apparently, they were with some friends at the town park last night. They decided to go swimming in the lake. They all got a little daring and decided to dive into the lake. I guess the kids who dived first were fine. When Alison tried it, she went in the water and never came back up. Some of the boys dove in after her. They started CPR. I'm not sure of all the details after that. The kids are still in shock."

"Oh my God," said Johnny. "What about Alison? Where is she?"

"She didn't make it, Johnny," said Mrs. Napolitano. "Alison is dead."

After those words were spoken, a long period of silence followed. No one was quite sure what to say. If they should say anything at all. My mind raced back in time to when we were all younger. We would play kickball every day after school. Sometimes, Alison would bring her Barbie dolls over to play with my sister, Rose. How could she be gone?

"Maybe we should go inside everybody," said my father. "We have some things to discuss."

"Yes, I'm sure this changes your plans," said Mrs. Napolitano. "I should go check on Laura and Matthew, too."

"Considering everything that has happened, I assume you kids will want to stay close to home?" My father looked at all the faces surrounding the kitchen table. There was a brief silence.

"I say we go," said Johnny. "It's only for the weekend. I think it's just things like this. I mean when something like this happens."

"It makes you think about time." Grandpa Frank answered in a clear, strong voice. "It makes you realize time is precious and just because you are young doesn't mean you have an abundance of it. If you can understand that Johnny at your age, than you will have a very full life. You will make every minute count. Not by doing foolish things, but doing things that make a difference. A person you are proud to be and others are proud to know. That's all there is to know about life. So many people make life so complicated. This world gets so busy with people running here and there. When I left Italy, my father took my hand. He said Frank, I am proud to call you my son. Make sure you live a good life in America, so you can say the same thing to your son. Every generation represents the generation before. Why would you do anything to shame all my years of hard work and love for my family."

"I think what Grandpa Frank is telling you is just to think before you act," said my mother. "Kids today don't think about tomorrow. They don't think about how their actions affect so many other people.

"I think a camping trip would be a good idea," I said. "After all, it's probably the last time we will all be together."

"Okay," said my father. "Whoever wants to come along with me and Grandpa Frank can grab their things. And if you don't, Grandpa and I will understand."

"That was the last camping trip we were all together."

"What?" asked my father.

"That day, when Alison died and we decided to still go on the camping trip. After that, nothing was ever the same. Everyone kind of went their own ways."

"Everyone started to become adults. And that means everyone makes choices of how to live their life. When you're a child, everything is pretty much told to you. When you become an adult, you have to decide for yourself. That doesn't mean just doing what your friends are doing."

"I thought Peter went on to college? Wasn't he valedictorian of his high school class?"

"Yes. He buried himself in books after his sister died. His parents thought he was fine. I don't think they talked about Alison much after she passed. Your mother would always invite Mrs. D'Agostino over for some tea, but she hardly ever said yes. Something happened to that boy in college. He came home one summer and never went back to school. I don't think he has a job. Your mother and I don't really talk to them anymore. I don't think anyone in the neighborhood does. I'll be surprised if they attend the funeral."

"Well, I know what Grandpa Frank would tell Peter if he were alive."

"It's probably the same thing Mr. & Mrs. Nuccio say to him."

"Mr. & Mrs. Nuccio. I almost forgot about them. Are they still alive? I can't believe they are still here in the neighborhood."

"I think they came with the neighborhood."

"I wonder if they still can dance?"

"I think their dancing days are over."

"I remember those block parties. Sure wish we had a video camera back then."

The end of summer in 1979...which meant the famous neighborhood block party must be near. In that year, we had the party at the end of August, right before school started. I was entering the third grade. The block party was famous for people just eating all day, sharing laughs, and dancing. The music was a lot of the greatest hits from the '50s and '60's and a little bit of the classics from Tony Bennett and Dean Martin. This year, some of the teenagers won the approval to play a little of the present hits. Billy Joel's album, "Just the Way You Are", would be blasting from the speakers too. It was a time when the most controversial show on television was 'All in the Family'. In a few months, we would all be asking 'Where is Iran?' and 'Why did they take Americans hostage?'

"Hello Little Elizabeth." Grandpa Frank pulled some coins out of his pocket. All the grandchildren came running.

"Dad, don't keep giving them money all the time."

"This is more than money. You don't spend this coin my bambinos. This coin will be worth more than a dollar someday. It is a special Susan B. Anthony coin they make this year. The man at the bank told me so."

"I won't spend it Grandpa." I ran with my cousin Johnny to get some corn on the cob.

"Who is this Susan lady?" asked Johnny.

"I don't know. But she must be important to have her face on money. Where is Matthew?"

"I see him over there standing with his mom. Come on, let's go get him."

"Hey Mattie!" yelled Johnny, as we ran over.

"Really Maggie, it's a great movie. You and Vincent should have a date night and go see it. I'll watch the kids for you," said Mrs. Napolitano.

"I'll think about it. You say this 'Kramer vs. Kramer' is about divorce though. I can't see how that would be much fun."

"What's that?" asked Mattie.

"It's the wave of the future," interrupted Mrs. Nuccio with a laugh. "I hear about more and more couples calling it quits. It's the kids that suffer. I don't know what this world is coming too. In my days, people took their vows seriously."

"And they took dancing seriously too," interrupted Mr. Nuccio. "Come on girl! Let's show these kids how it's done."

"I hope we're as active as that in our senior years," exclaimed Mrs. Napolitano.

"Just look at those two." My dad walked over to my mom. They watched Mr. & Mrs. Nuccio dance to Dean Martin singing, 'You're Nobody Till Somebody Loves You'.

"They're pretty good for old people," Johnny said. I nodded my head in agreement.

"You guys want to go on a bike ride tomorrow?" asked Matthew. "It might be our last chance before stupid school starts. We can check out that new dish thing your dad was talking about just up the big hill."

"Yeah." Johnny agreed. "And let's bring a lunch and stay gone the whole day. We'll be like explorers."

"Explorers with a dog to keep away any trouble," interrupted Johnny's father, my Uncle Joseph.

"I don't know if I want them riding that far on their bikes."

"Don't worry Maggie," answered my father. "I'll ask Timmy to call you when they pass his farm on West Street. If you musketeers have any problems, you stop at his house, capisce?"

"Yes dad," I answered and gave him a hug. "I can't wait for tomorrow to come. Grandpa Frank, we are going on a bike ride tomorrow to see the big dish."

"What's this big dish?"

"Pop, it's a satellite dish for that new sports broadcast station, ESPN.

"Sports all the time? Who has time to sit home and watch sports all day?"

"I think it will be nice to have on the weekend."

"No Joseph," my Grandpa Frank answered loudly. He gave his son a whack on the back of his head. Johnny, Matthew and me giggled. "You spend time with family."

"You tell them," interrupted Mr. Nuccio, as he walked over with Mrs. Nuccio. "These young men are wasting all their youthful energy just standing here with their pretty wives. Not one of them has danced. Come on now, everybody."

Johnny, Matthew and I watched all the old people dance and giggled at their funny dance moves. We ate spumoni and talked about our exciting adventure planned for tomorrow.

The next morning, we all met in front of Mr. Ferrucci's store. We bought some candy and soda to go with the nutritious lunches our mothers had packed. We hopped on our bikes and pedaled past Goat's Island and the railroad tracks. The ride up Daniel's Farm Hill Road was happily greeted with the long stretch of flat road on West Street. Johnny's dog, Captain, eagerly ran alongside us. We approached the big white dish.

"I can see it," shouted Matthew. We cruised our bikes down the hill towards this new building called ESPN.

"Wow! That sucker is huge," exclaimed Johnny.

"I think it's kind of ugly."

We stopped from a short distance to take in the view.

"I agree with Elizabeth." Tim, the sheep man, walked up to us and leaned against his fence. "My sheep don't like all the traffic that place is creating. It won't be long before you kids won't be able to ride your bikes on West Street."

"There's always Queen Street, with all those cows," said Johnny.

"Queen Street with all those cows."

"You say something?" asked my dad. He sat behind the wheel and started the car.

"I was just thinking about Queen Street and all the cows that used to be there."

"All those cows are now Big Macs and Whoppers."

"Thanks for the visual."

"Always here to provide assistance." My father began the drive to Aunt Sophia's house. It was time for the family dinner.

Family Dinner

"Well, if it ain't the city girl!" said my quick-witted cousin Tommy.

"You know, I probably see more trees and wildlife than you do here in suburbanville Southington."

"Yes, Elizabeth has a place in up-state New York that she spends almost every weekend at," interrupted my mother.

"I'm sure Steinbeck must love it there too." My sister entered the kitchen and gave me a hug. "I better hug you now while I can. Only four more months to go."

"Congrats on baby number two. Having any more after this?"

"I don't think so. Two is enough for me, and our checking account."

"That's why I like Steinbeck. He only eats twice a day and I give him a bath once a month."

"Who's watching the smartest dog in the world while you're here?" asked my mother.

"My friend Max has Steinbeck at his place. I'm sure he has already taken him for walks in Central Park at least a dozen times by now."

"You have a friend named Max?"

"I see your hearing aid is working well, Aunt Caterina. And that dress is very pretty. Is it new?"

"Oh, this old thing."

"It just looks new, because she only wears it to wakes," smirked her husband, Dominick. "Lately, she has been wearing it too often. It seems like yesterday your Grandpa Frank was bouncing little Elizabeth on his knee, while sitting under his grapevine."

"At least we will all have some time to listen to a few great memories that Grandpa Frank has given us at the funeral."

"Oh really, Rose. Who's doing a speech?"

"It's called a eulogy and mom said you are."

"That's news to me. Especially since I don't give speeches."

"Eulogy."

"Whatever you call it. It is still standing in front of people and talking for a long time."

"It doesn't have to be that long."

"It's not going to be anything. When will I even have time to write something?"

"You have two days and stop worrying. No one is looking for perfection."

"No, but it has to be good. I mean I would want it to be good. Where is mom? I love how she conveniently slips away."

"Yes, mothers are good at that." Uncle Dominick tried to ease the tension in our conversation. "I'm sure your Grandpa Frank will love whatever you say about him. And what's to be nervous about. It's just family."

Just family, I thought to myself as we all sat in Aunt Sophia's gigantic dining room. The table was long enough to sit all my grandmother's sisters and their husbands, my aunts and uncles, at least half of my cousins and their spouses. A few screaming infants make the seating arrangement complete. Any leftover relatives sat at a few small round tables placed strategically by the aunts. Each aunt could be designated a table for interrogation, or just eavesdropping. I walked in the room and tried to make a dash for a small round table. Grandma Marie waved her hand and motioned to sit by her. This wasn't so bad, as I was closer to the wine bottles. I had a feeling I would need a drink to survive this family dinner. I sat down and looked around the table at all these people who were somehow related to me. It always surprised me how most of us have family, whom if they weren't related, would probably never choose that person as a friend. As my Grandpa Frank would say, 'The Lord giveth, and then he laughs his ass off when he sees the look of horror on your face.' I wouldn't say I have a look of horror on my face when I see the cousins that God has provided me with. I guess it's just a look of wonder.

My cousins are all married and live a very typical suburban Connecticut lifestyle. They have homes that are too big for them. Garages that contain leased cars under the family business. They work long hours to afford the expensive house. This forced them to put their children in day-care, which brought on the guilt of not spending enough time with their children. Therefore, a family vacation is planned once a year, which they charge and then spend the next few months trying to pay off. My cousins were in no way raised with the kind of lifestyle they live today. I often wonder why they strive for it now. One might say, maybe they are happy? I ponder the question and ask, if they are so happy being apart from their family so much, why did they have one? My grandfather and I would often go for walks in the cemetery. He would tell me stories of the friends and family who were buried there. I remember something he told me one summer day at the age of twenty-two. I was wondering if I had made the right choices in my life. Not following the family business. He stopped walking and held my face in his hands....

"Ah...this ageing up is more difficult than you thought Elizabeth?" asked my Grandpa Frank. We walked through the cemetery on a summer evening in 1993.

"Growing up, Grandpa. I think you mean growing up."

"Yes, yes. You know my English is not as good as yours. I do not think talking is as important as listening. Capisce?"

"So, I should just listen to my heart when making choices in my life?"

"No, those words are for the movie screen. Remember when you told your parents you did not want to go into the family business?"

"Yes, and you were there backing me up. You said it is important for people to follow their dreams, their passion."

"Yes. I remember the sound of your voice when you told your parents your dreams. Your voice did not quiver, your eyes looked straight into theirs and you were persistent in making them understand. You had made the choice that was right for you and you were ready."

"Yeah, I knew exactly what I wanted and I had a plan to get there with or without them."

"You were confident. You sounded confident. Yes, you had this plan you say. You had a dream. Many people have dreams and make a plan, but then they stop," Grandpa Frank slapped his hands together. "They stop because of fear. They let this fear show and people stop believing in them. Then the dream just stops. They may do what other people say is best or safe. Then other pains in your head come to you."

"Other pains?"

"Do you know what I would be doing if I stayed in Italy? I would be building beautiful homes for other people. I knew I wanted to build a home for me, and that would never happen if I stayed in Italy. My father said, 'Why don't you go to America? That place is filled with dreamers.' Well, you know the rest."

"Weren't you scared?"

"I was damn scared. But I knew what I wanted. I told my father, with passion and confidence, I would not be staying with my brothers in the business. Marie and I were going to America. You see, Elizabeth? I say it with such confidence that my father started to think this America may be o.k."

"Even though I still am scared, I am doing the right thing?"

"Do not ask the question. Say it like, even though I am scared, I am going to follow my dream. I have plan. I have passion. I do not want to do anything else. I go, to work hard, to live my dream."

"I have passion. I have confidence. And I have no pain in the head!"

"Funny, Miss I was born in America, and should have a little respect for the Grandpa who sailed on a boat for days, with only enough food to eat once a day."

"Oh, it's a boat now. Last week it was a raft." I laughed and put my hand in his as we continued to walk in the cemetery. "So tell me what are these other pains in the head I will get if I don't follow my dream?"

"Your Grandma calls them window pains."

44

"Grandpa, I think-"

"Now hush, don't interrupt an old man. You see, when people look at their life, it's like looking out your window. You see everything you have accomplished, and you realize that other people can see your accomplishments too. They can look inside your window. The person who was never sure if they made the right choice, or even worse, too scared to follow their dream. This person is always wondering if the view from their window is good enough. They start to look at the view from other peoples' windows and try to have the same view, or maybe even better. These people get so busy looking out other peoples' windows they forget to create their own beautiful view. But, they can't do that anymore."

"Why not?"

"Because they are not sure what makes them happy. They are so busy following what is making everybody else happy. They forget about the passion you need to live life. Passion is doing what brings you joy and you don't care if anybody is looking. You have to keep doing it, because it completes you and you are confident in who you are. When a soul loses this passion, they turn away from all the reasons they were placed here by God. Never lose your passion, Elizabeth. The person with passion doesn't worry what everybody has for a view. They are so in love with the view of their own. When you spend time away from living your passion, you try to fill this pain you get from looking at the view from another's window. Soon you spend all your time filling this pain with what others say will make you happy. It will not work. It may change the view from your window, but it will not change your true passion in life. It will always yearn in your heart."

"Elizabeth, pass the gravy," said my cousin Nick.

"Huh, oh yeah."

"Maybe she's working on her next novel. All in her head, before she writes it down."

"Nice cufflinks." Nick reached to take the gravy from my hands.

"They better be nice. They cost enough money. The designer has the best reputation in Manhattan. It's the only place I buy my jewelry."

"Really," said another cousin. "I was thinking of getting a new pair."

"They really provide a nice view. Was buying a new pair of cufflinks something you were passionate about?"

"Huh?"

"It's nothing. Forget it. But I think they inspired me with something to share when I say Grandpa Frank's eulogy."

"Oh, that is wonderful." Grandma Marie took my hand. "You see, family and good food always bring out the best in people."

"Well, the food sure is good." My mother gave me a glare and quickly changed the subject.

"Uncle Dominick, how do the grapes look this year?"

"Excellent, as always. The wine for next year's Christmas will be one of the best. Since some of the grapes will come from Frank's grapevine, it will be like he is still with us. Salute everybody."

After a pause, my mother spoke. "I was only asking because I was planning to make some jam."

"Yeah right," said a few of my cousins in unison, with huge smiles.

"Now, now," said my Uncle Dominick. "I remember when Margaret's jam saved Frank and I from a little situation."

"You were supposed to be watching the grandkids go ice skating."

"Yes Caterina, and that we were. As I recall, it was Frank and me and Geno and you Rocco. You were part of this ice skating club too."

"Oh yes, all the brother-in-laws were there for the wine tasting....err...ice-skating party." Rocco was a quiet man who liked to mostly eat at these family get togethers. He was married to my Grandma Marie's sister, Rosetta, a fabulous cook.

"Yes, all the old Italian men were there," Grandma Marie interrupted. "You were supposed to be watching my precious grandchildren."

My grandparents have three children: Vincent, Joe and Mary. They have nine grandchildren. My Uncle Joseph and Aunt Betty have three kids: Johnny, Joe Jr. and Nick. My Aunt Mary and Uncle Steve have four kids: Laura, Beth, Katherine and Tommy. Of course my father and mother, Vincent and Margaret, have just two kids: my sister Rose and me.

"And watching your grandchildren, we were. I remember it well...."

"Another February in Connecticut. I don't know if my bones can take another winter." Dominick complained to his brother-in-laws. They sat on a bench and watched Frank's grandchildren ice skate.

"Well, you can say you survived another blizzard. The blizzard of '76," replied Geno.

"Yeah," interrupted Rocco. "I have a mountain of snow in my driveway."

"All right Frank, what's keeping that smile on your face?" asked Geno.

"I am just enjoying watching my grandchildren, instead of listening to old men complain."

"Hey, you're the one who told us to come to the park!"

"Well, there wasn't much choice Geno. Come here, or stay at my house with that hen party going on." Rocco was referring to all the sisters' monthly get together for lunch and gossip.

"What do you think they talk about?" questioned Dominick.

"How lucky they are to be married to such good looking men," laughed Geno.

"You must have taking a few sips of wine before walking here."

"No, but I wish I had. I can't feel my toes."

"How about some jam?"

"Jam, Frank? What good is jam going to do?"

"I packed some jam and crackers for my grandchildren. They love our home-made jam. It comes from the best grapevine in America. Here, I make you some."

Frank passed each of his brother-in-laws a cracker with jam. They all ate the cracker with jam and agreed it was very good. "Maybe, you would all like a little drink to wash it down, yes?" He reached into the bag again, and pulled out another jam jar. It contained Grandpa Frank's homemade wine.

"Now this is a way to spend a Saturday afternoon."

"Give me that jar, Rocco. I am the one with the frozen toes."

They all had a drink from the jar. Frank quickly snatched the wine from Dominick and placed it in the box. Just as Rocco was about to complain, he was interrupted.

"Hello gentlemen," said Sergeant O'Riley. "Are we enjoying a day with the grandkids Frank?"

"Hello Patrick. Why I remember when I could bounce you on my knee. Time sure goes by fast....especially at my age."

"Ah, you look just as fit and handsome as when I was a little boy. What's your secret?"

"Spending time with young people," Grandpa Frank gestured to his grandkids, skating on the pond.

"Yes, they certainly have a lot of energy at that age. And they get hungry, too. I suppose that is why you brought along this box of food?"

"Yes. Have you ever tried my wife's jam? Go ahead, take a jar and I'll get you a cracker."

"Well, I don't mind if I do." Sergeant O'Riley reached into the box. The brother-in-laws watched his hand with a look of tension.

"The lid may be a little tight, but I'm sure they keep you fit at the police station."

"But of course." Sergeant O'Riley unscrewed the lid and raised the jar to his nose.

"Well, are you going to smell it or taste it," laughed Grandpa Frank, as he offered him a cracker.

"Yes, thank you." He dipped the cracker in the jar and was able to scoop some jam on it. "Delicious. Tell Mrs. Manciano this is the best jam I have ever tasted."

"I certainly will. Make sure you don't stay outside to long. A man can get frostbite awfully fast out here."

"Yes. I was on my way to check the other park by the apple orchard."

"Very good. Nice to know the children are being so protected by our police officers."

Sergeant O'Riley walked back to his car and drove away. All the men waved as he drove past.

"That was close." Dominick gave a sigh of relief.

"Those young kids put a uniform on and think they know everything. Doesn't he know this is the Italian side of town."

"Sure he does, Rocco. That's why he came here to get a drink. Everyone knows Italians make the best wine." Grandpa Frank pulled out the jar of wine. "Here's to Italian men everywhere. May we always be better at everything than those Irish immigrants."

"Salute!" they all replied.

Everyone at the table laughed as Uncle Dominick told the story. I could picture my cousins and I ice skating on that day and looking over at my Grandpa Frank. He always seemed to have all the time in the world for me. My parents were always busy, but I could always ride my bike to Grandpa Frank's home. He would sit with me under his grapevine, and listen to my problems. I'm sure my adolescent problems were so easy to fix, but he never really told me how to fix them. I guess that's why I preferred to talk to him, instead of my parents. My folks would let me talk, and then provide a solution to quickly make the hurt go away. Not my Grandpa Frank. He would look me in the eyes when I spoke, and listened to every word I said. I knew he was listening, because the stories he would tell me afterwards always involved a lesson learned from someone else who had the similar problem. As an adult, I now realize that other person having the same problems was my Grandpa Frank, when he was a little boy. Grandpa Frank always said everybody in this world has the same problems and fears. Sometimes they are just wrapped differently. Everyone wants to be loved, respected and listened to. Maybe that's what made Grandpa Frank so special to me. He always loved me, respected me and was never too busy to listen to me. Maybe it's also those qualities that made the hurt from my problems go away, not simply providing a solution. I remember one visit to his grapevine when all I wanted was a solution...

"Yes, that is a difficult spot to be in. Not that I would know of course, being a boy."

"I know you're a boy, Grandpa. So, what do you think I should do?"

"Hmmm. When is this junior prom?"

"A month from Friday. But I need time to get a dress and all that stuff."

"Yes, all that stuff."

"And I need to let the guys know which one I'll be going with."

"Yes, yes," interrupted Grandpa Frank, "that would be the honorable thing to do."

"Are you making fun of me?"

"Honorable. That word reminds me of a time when I was speaking to my father back in the old country." Grandpa Frank rubbed his chin and took another sip from his wine glass. He swirled the wine in his glass while gazing into it like a crystal ball. "My father was a stern man. He worked hard every day of his life and always had enough food on the table and a place for his family to live. When I was leaving for America with your Grandma Marie, I asked him if he had any advice for me. He looked me in the eyes and said, 'if you always do what is honorable, you will always do the right thing'. Sometimes that was difficult and sometimes it seemed like I was the only honorable one. You must remember this Elizabeth. Someday, you will get old like me. You will have the time to sit and think about your life. It is very good to sit and do that with a smile. And a glass of wine, of course."

"But Grandpa, you make it sound like a life or death decision. I'm not moving to a new country. I just have two dates to the junior prom and I need to get rid of one."

"Life or death? No. But maybe it is all these little decisions that will help you make a big decision someday. Why do you think God makes you be a teenager, capicse?"

"I guess I should go with Kevin. We have been friends for so long. I would be helping him out. His girlfriend dumped him last week. But the other guy is so cute."

"Yes, cute, dainty... I think the dictionary says."

"Say, getting scholarly are we?"

"I read. I teach myself when I come to this country. You kids get a free education and you don't appreciate it. Sink up all the knowledge you can."

"Soak up."

"Yes, soak up. Aghhh! Do you want to hear how handsome I was in my youth or not?"

"You still are handsome, Grandpa Frank."

"That's because handsome means dignified; it takes a very honorable person to stay dignified...yes? You see what I am trying to say Elizabeth? Your Grandma Marie trusted to come with me to America. She knew I would always do what is best for us and our family. I would never shame her. I would always be a handsome man to her." He puffed on his cigar. "Elizabeth, which man do you want to be seen with- a cute one or a handsome one? A man who will be fun, fun fun? or a man who will be good to you?"

"Why not find one who is both things?"

"Never happen," snapped back Grandpa Frank.

"Why not? I think you are fun and cute and honorable and handsome, all at the same time." I put my arm around him and gave him a kiss.

"It will never happen, because I am from the old country. They don't make men like me in America. I think it has something to do with the water. That's why I only drink wine."

We both laughed. Grandpa Frank let me take a sip from his glass. He let me do that now and then, but I had to promise to never tell my Grandma Marie. She thought all my babies would be born with two heads if I drank at such a young age. Especially Grandpa Frank's wine. Grandpa Frank would just laugh and say, 'two heads are better than one.'

I did go with my friend Kevin to the junior prom. We had a lot of fun. As far as the cute guy, I don't even remember his name. I have no idea what happened to him after graduation. Kevin and me, we still send Christmas cards and e-mails now and then. He is a very dignified family man and highly respected in his community. I have taken his financial advice in the past and trust him to always give me an honest answer. I guess you could say he is a very handsome man. Thanks for the advice Grandpa Frank....I miss you.

While most of the family members were sitting at the table trying to solve all the world problems, I was able to escape. I graciously took some empty plates to the kitchen. My Grandma Marie was washing the good china.

"Grandma, you know you can buy plates that are dishwasher safe. Then, you won't have to stand here and do all these dishes."

"Yes, but then I would have to sit at the table and listen to those men who think they should be president. Besides, I like washing dishes. Washing dishes will help you solve any problem you have."

"Oh really?"

"Frank and I would always end any argument we had while we were washing dishes. It's impossible to stay mad at someone you really love, when you are forced to stand beside them and wash the dishes for a family of five. So, one person would say a little something and then the next person would say a little something and then we were talking."

"Yes, but who talks first?"

"I don't remember. When you really love someone you don't keep score."

"Maybe you should write a book Grandma. You can call it, How to Save Your Marriage by Washing Dishes at Twilight."

"See that pan? That dirty one."

"Yeah, are you going to make me clean that? It's going to take forever."

"No, it won't take forever. But it will take time and some muscle, yes?"

"Yes," I said with a moan.

"That dirty pan is just like life. It will take time to get it clean. Sometimes you may ask yourself why you cooked anything in the pan, because it is a pain to get clean. Then you remember the joy on peoples' faces when they ate the food. How you enjoyed their company while sharing the food. Then, the little bother of cleaning the pan, it does not seem like such a bother anymore. You see, I clean the pan while we were talking. Look at that shine. All ready for the next family dinner."

"Any other pans need cleaning?"

"You don't worry about this. Why don't you go sit with your Aunts in the parlor? They would love to hear about New York City."

"Do they know there are no longer any chickens in Brooklyn?"

"You hush...and be nice. Tell them of all the things you write about."

"Oh, this should be interesting." I entered the parlor of doom.

"There she is." Aunt Sophia gestured to sit next to her. "Do you notice anything special about the parlor Elizabeth?"

As I looked around with my hand on my chin, Aunt Caterina leaned over and said, "...no plastic on the furniture."

They started to laugh all together. Aunt Rosetta moved her chair closer and said, "I remember when your Grandpa Frank said, 'Sophia, I bet when I die you still won't take the plastic off the parlor furniture.' You see, I remembered girls."

"So, tell us all your exciting adventures in New York City."

"Well, I'm sure the city has changed somewhat since you were all little girls. But I think the feeling of being in Manhattan hasn't changed. The excitement of getting dressed up to see a play on Broadway, catching a cab to Little Italy to share a great meal with friends until the early morning hours. Walking through Central Park after the first snowfall, or on a quiet summer night. I think the feelings experienced in those moments are the same with each generation."

"So well put...don't you think so?" Aunt Caterina looked at her sisters. "Just listening to you, takes me back to the first apartment Dominick and I had in Brooklyn. We were so proud of ourselves. I kept that place spotless, from the floors to the windows to the front steps. In those days, people took pride in where they lived; even if it was an apartment. Not like today. I don't know if I'd want to see that place today. Probably looks like a mess."

"I don't get to Brooklyn much. Actually, I do a lot of traveling to research my stories. Most of the time, I'm not in New York. I love traveling, and Steinbeck loves it too."

"Oh, who's Steinbeck?" asked an inquisitive Aunt Caterina.

"He's my dog." My Aunts looked on with a hint of disappointment. "Steinbeck and I get along great on the road. He's actually a great icebreaker when I go on interviews. We were just in South Dakota and did a lot of hiking together. I was working on a tourism article for a travel magazine. I'm sure my Grandma will show it to you when it's published."

"Oh yes, your grandparents are so proud of you." Aunt Rosetta paused, remembering I only have a grandma now. "I will miss your Grandpa Frank calling Rocco over to his grapevine. He would always share a magazine that would have your writings, and smile so wide. Your Grandpa taught himself to read English, just like we all did when we came to America."

"We had to in those days. None of this free money or special rules like they have today," interrupted my Uncle Rocco. "In our times, you learned fast to survive and to be able to support your family. We didn't take charity. We just worked hard. No time to complain or feel sorry for yourself. After all, we were in America, the land of opportunity. And look at us now. We have house, healthy families and a famous writer in Aunt Sophia's parlor."

"Oh, thanks for the honorable mention."

"Marie says you are working with a famous photographer, yes?" asked Aunt Caterina.

"Uh...a photographer, yes. I don't know about the famous part."

"I have a camera," interrupted Uncle Dominick. "Yep, works beautifully."

"You have a Polaroid camera from 1975, and you're too cheap to buy a new one." Caterina answered back, while giving him a poke in the ribs.

"It still takes great pictures. What type of camera does this famous photographer use?"

"His name is Max and he mostly uses digital cameras. That way, you can see your photo right away."

"Oh yes. These kids got to have everything right away."

"Well, it's important that he gets a great picture, or he doesn't get paid, Uncle Dominick."

"People make good money for just taking pictures. Hey Rocco, maybe you and I should take my Polaroid and smack the open road."

"It's 'hit the open road'."

"Ah, so it is."

I just leaned back in my chair and listened to Uncle Rocco and Uncle Dominick laugh. Their laugh was so similar to Grandpa Frank's it gave me goose bumps. I wonder if my Grandma Marie had the same goose bumps on her arms. I started to remember how I would never hear my Grandpa Frank laugh again. My eyes started to tear up. My mother came over, and put her arm around me.

"You two men have a very thievery laugh. Whenever I heard Grandpa Frank laugh like that, I would always wonder if he was laughing at something that just happened, or if there was something more amusing that we all didn't see," shared my mother.

"Hmmm, I can recall a time when Frank walked around the house for a week with a crinkled smile and a consistent chuckle. I never dreamed he could have planned what he did that year in 1988." Grandma Marie seemed to be visualizing one of the happiest days of her life.

"Are you sure they are on their way, Margaret?" asked my Aunt Mary. She told the D.J. to turn the music down a bit.

"Vincent said he would have them here exactly at 1:00. He told his parents I was taking the girls shopping for Easter dresses and he wanted to take them out to lunch."

"I see them. They just pulled into the parking lot," shouted my Uncle Joe. He told everybody at the banquet hall to be quiet.

Suddenly the doors opened and all 200 guests started to cheer. It was the first time I saw my Grandpa and Grandma as a couple. I was seventeen years old and, to me, those two old people were just my grandparents. They had always been grandparents, in my eyes, and were always together. That day, I saw them look at each other as best friends....two people just wanting to make the other person feel as happy as they do....just because. How great it must be to find someone who wants to make you happy just because. My grandparents kissed and everyone started shouting 'Speech! Speech!' My Grandpa Frank took the microphone from the D.J. and the room became quiet.

"I just awant to say....in the best English I know how," my Grandpa Frank paused, and took his best girl's hand in his, "....I just want everyone to know that this is my one and only and I hope....my wish for all a'you young people out there is that someday you will have a love like I found....and for you not so young, butta not so old..." there was an interruption of laughter and then Grandpa Frank continued, "...I hope you hold every day close to your heart and keep your love happy and good. And to my wife Marie....I hope we have another fifty years of being happy and good....salute!" They kissed, and everybody drank from their wine glasses. The D.J. started to play Dean Martin, 'You're Nobody Till Somebody Loves You.'

I danced with all my cousins that day and we ate and drank from one in the afternoon until we were forced to leave the banquet facility at seven o'clock that night. My grandparents were surprised with a trip to Niagara Falls. The limousine was waiting to take them to the airport. Their honeymoon...after fifty years of marriage. I wondered what it must be like to be married for fifty years. I've seen my grandparents bicker at each other, but it never felt like they hated each other. I was sure there were times when they were bored with each other, because I've seen them wash dishes together and never say a word. They were always together. They were my grandparents. That's what they were supposed to do.

"Have you decided what you are going to say?"

"Huh," I stammered, as I brought myself back to my Aunt Sophia's parlor.

"Have you decided what you are going to say?" asked my Aunt Caterina.

"You mean at the funeral?"

"Yes dear...have you written anything yet? We are expecting a lot of people at the wake, and who knows how many are attending the funeral."

"I'm sure Elizabeth has it all under control," said Uncle Dominick. "Just keep it short."

"And funny," added Uncle Rocco.

"But meaningful. Tell some stories about your Grandpa Frank, people will like that," advised Aunt Sophia.

"Your Grandpa was such a special man. Just make it as special as he was. No one could ask for more," included Aunt Rosetta.

Great. I need to write a speech in one day that is short, funny, meaningful and as special as my Grandpa Frank. Then, stand in front of friends, relatives and a priest and present myself in a calm and dignified manner while speaking in front of a casket. All my worst fears wrapped up in one day. Who could ask for more?

Pre-Funeral Jitters

I paced the hardwood floor in my old bedroom. My brain did not seem to be working this morning. I had one day to write this eulogy for Grandpa Frank. 'I think my nerves are affecting my ability to write,' I spoke out loud as my father walked by in the hallway.

"What's the matter, kiddo?"

"I just can't do this. I just don't know how to say what I want to say. I mean I know what I want to say, but it just doesn't come out when I try to say it. Aghhhh!"

"Maybe that's because you're thinking too much instead of just talking. You always said writing is just like talking. So, just talk to yourself."

"I know. It's just when I sit in front of my laptop, I go blank."

"There's an easy solution to that. Don't sit in front of your laptop."

"Cute, very cute. I'm glad you can find the humor in this. Meanwhile, I have to give a speech tomorrow in front of millions of people."

"Wow. I didn't know St. Thomas Church could hold millions of people."

"Well, to me it will seem like a million. And I have nothing to say."

"I thought you just said, you know what you want to say. Are you sure you went to college. I know I paid the tuition."

"Aren't you going somewhere?"

"Yeah, more relatives to see. Want to come along?"

"No. I don't need any more relatives giving me advice on the eulogy."

"I'm positive these relatives will only give you the advice you want to hear, or sometimes need to hear, or is that- think you need to hear. Oh, just grab your jacket."

I sat in my dad's pick-up truck, as he placed a few things in the back. The neighborhood was quiet. I love getting up early in the morning and feeling like you are waking up the world. I love watching the sunrise and not knowing what the day will bring, but still excited about all the endless possibilities. My dad enjoyed this same time of day. It gave us our own little 'bonding time' together when I was a kid. The truck turned right, and I realized we were entering the cemetery. It seemed a lot more crowded with headstones since the last time I'd been here.

"The place is booming."

"The prices are booming, too. It's amazing what the Church gets away with these days. Actually charging people to be buried. You should buy a plot now before the price increases."

"Now dad, you know I'm not going in the ground."

"I don't want to hear it. Hopefully, I'll be gone before you and won't have to know about it."

"I'll be sure my cremation experience is the first thing we talk about in Heaven."

"How will I know it's you? You will be all burnt."

"Funny dad, really funny!"

We carried the shovels and flowers to the family plot. I looked at all the names of my ancestors on the footstones. They all seemed to live long lives, at least for in those days. Most lived until their late sixties, except a few uncles who died in the war.

"You think they were bored?"

"Bored...who?"

"Our relatives. Do you think they were bored? I mean they lived and died in Southington. They never had a chance to really do anything."

"Well, what about your grandparents? They came over from Italy and it wasn't a luxury cruise ship."

"I know that. But after that. They just settled, you know?"

"They settled into a nice home and raised their kids and made sure they went to school and learned how to speak and read English. Then those kids grew and got married and had kids and those kids actually finished high school. They got good jobs and nice homes too, so they could raise their kids and...hey, that would be you. So, what's your next move big shot?"

"My move? I've already moved to New York, remember."

"Aren't you bored, just living and writing in the city every day?"

"How can you say that? I'm doing what I love."

"Then I guess the answer is no."

"No?"

"No, they weren't bored. They were doing what they loved."

"But how do you know that?"

"Well, I never heard them complain. Pass me the spade."

"Well, maybe they never complained because they didn't know what they were missing."

"Or maybe they were so content, they never gave a second thought to what they might be missing."

"How do you know that?"

"How do I know what?"

"Agh! You're stalling to think of an answer. How do you know they were content?"

"A person knows they're content when they don't worry about what everybody else is doing. The problem with your generation is you are so busy looking at what everybody else is doing. Your own life is passing you by. Your grandparents came to America and lived their American dream. They didn't need to read a book or listen to the radio to decide what their dream should be. They just listened to each other and followed their hearts. They made their dream come true. So, they were content. Stop making life so difficult to understand."

"That sounds like something Grandpa would say."

"Is that something you think he would say, or something you just needed to hear?"

"Oh, you're so smart. Pass me the marigolds." 'Marigolds,' I whispered to myself, as my mind took me back to 1976.

"Elizabeth, come help your Grandpa. We have much to do today." He placed a tray of flowers in my five year old arms.

"Grandpa, why do you have so many flowers?"

"Elizabeth, this is a very special year. This is the bicentennial of our country. Oh yes, we must celebrate this very special Fourth of July."

"Will we have fireworks?"

"Oh yes, fireworks. Mr. Ferrucci has promised to have some fireworks for us at his store. You help me plant the flowers this morning. Then, we go see Mr. Ferrucci after lunch. Sound good Elizabeth?"

"Yes Grandpa. And maybe Mr. Ferrucci will have some candy?"

"Yes, some candy too."

Grandpa Frank sat down near his grapevine and faced the trolley tracks. "All the people that ride the trolley will see our beautiful flowers and remember that this is a special year. You see the flowers your Grandma and I bought? Do you notice something about them?"

"Well, they are red, white and blue. Just like our flag."

"That's good Elizabeth. You see how smart you are getting. And you didn't want to go to school...tsk! tsk!"

"Well, I like being with you instead."

"Yes, well I like being with you, too. So let's enjoy our day, yes? Now, the flowers we must plant before they weld."

"It's wilt, Dad," answered my father, as he approached my Grandpa and I with some more flowers in his hands.

"Oh Vincent. Never scare an old man like that."

"Show me an old man."

"You see Elizabeth? Your father gets his sense of humor from me."

"Looks like you two have everything under control."

"We do have everything under control. Elizabeth and I were just getting ready to make the American Flag."

"That's a great idea, Dad. The people in the trolley will love it. I'm going to say hello to Mom and then I have a few errands to run. Elizabeth, you stay with Grandma and Grandpa until I come get you this afternoon, okay?"

"Okay. Grandpa and I are going to see Mr. Ferrucci after lunch."

"No candy, Dad."

"Of course no candy. I would never give the girl candy."

"You were just teasing, right Grandpa Frank?"

"Let's see how gooda job you do with these flowers. See the reds, we will start with the reds." He moved his hand along the dirt, and I followed while dropping the flowers in the dirt.

"Grandpa, you want me to put dirt around the flowers now?"

"Not yet, don't rush when you plant flowers. You plant flowers like you plant your life. You see, first you loosen the soil. You see if it's good to grow things here, not too many rocks to get in your way. Then, you arrange the flowers on the ground and take a few steps back like so and say, yes, all looks good. I wouldn't change a thing. Then, you cover the roots with a little dirt and give a little food and care and then you watch them grow." Grandpa Frank stepped back to admire the first planted row of flowers.

"And now I plant the white, Grandpa Frank?"

"Yes. You see, it gets easier as you go along, just like life. That first row you make, you must be very careful and have everything just so. Or everything else will not look so nice."

"I see a good job, and that means candy."

"Yes, candy at Mr. Ferrucci. But first, we finish the planting and Grandma will make us some lunch."

"Elizabeth, you want some lunch? Elizabeth?" My dad walked towards the tree I was sitting under, at the cemetery.

"Huh?"

"Lunch. It's almost noon, kiddo. We can get some free lunch at your Aunt's house, or we can go to-"

"The Apple Shack!" I shouted with a grin.

"I thought you might want to go there. And since I finished most of the work here by myself."

"Sorry dad, I guess my mind wandered."

"Your mind wandered when you were a little girl, too. Now, I guess you get paid to wander."

"Yes, so much pay that I'm buying lunch at the shack."

"Wow. Write this date down." My dad smirked, as we both got in the truck and slowly cruised out of the cemetery.

The Apple Shack was the biggest summer-time hangout when I was in high school. Most of the kids would stop there after returning from the beach for the day. It wasn't anything fancy; picnic tables and plenty of shade from the apple trees, and a few booths inside. The place got its name from all the apples that would drop from the tree and roll off the roof. Sometimes, an apple would land on your head, while you were sitting at the picnic table. My best friend Katy and I would order fried dough, french fries and two large sodas. I remember one day we had to place our order fairly quickly...

"Let's do it at the next light." Katy and I gave our friends in the car ahead of us the signal.

"Okay, the light just turned red...now!" Katy screamed, as we jumped out of the car and ran to our friends. They jumped out, too. We formed a huddle at the intersection, mooned the cars opposite us and then ran back to our vehicles. The light turned green and we were off.

"Whew. What a rush." I gave the thumbs up to our friends in the other car.

"Ummm, Elizabeth," said Katy, "...do you have any idea how long that cop car has been behind us?"

"What? He is kind of far....don't you think?"

"Well, let's get a little farther away." Katy increased her speed and we lost sight of him around the corner. We caught up to our friends and pulled alongside of their car.

"Cops," I screamed, "follow us!" We took off to the Apple Shack. We pulled into the parking lot. Katy and I placed a huge order for the gang. Everybody found a picnic table and tried to act casual.

"I didn't see a cop drive by yet," said our friend Vicki.

"Don't keep looking around like that. You look like you've got something to hide."

"Girls, you can get your drinks and the rest will be ready in a few minutes."

"Thanks Mr. D." We ran to get the drinks, and then set the table to make it look like we had been there awhile.

"Uh, oh....look who is driving by."

It was Officer Norton, one of the sleazy cops of Southington. I guess every town has a few of these, but Southington seemed to have a whole flock. You never wanted to be pulled over by one of the sleazy cops. They would look you up and down and try to intimidate you by sticking their face in yours. I guess part of their problem was boredom, since nothing exciting ever happened in Southington.

"Hello ladies." Officer Norton approached our table with his mirror sunglasses. "Are you enjoying your summer vacation?"

"Yes," we answered in unison, and took a sip from our sodas.

"Returning from the beach?"

"Yeah. Just getting some snack food before we call it a day," I answered. "I guess your son could tell you how exhausting it is lying at the beach all day."

Officer Norton's son had a lot of time to spend at the beach this summer, since he wasn't attending football camp. He came to our junior prom totally drunk and got into a lot of trouble. He had to choose between leaving the football team or the basketball team. Since his mom is having an affair with the basketball coach, and needs an excuse to attend the games to meet 'her squeeze', leaving the football team was strongly encouraged. Poor Officer Norton doesn't have a clue. Maybe he should take off those sunglasses.

"Well ladies, I guess I'm calling it a day too. My shift is up and I'm going home to have some lemonade with my wife."

"Oh, what a nice husband you are," responded Vicki, with a sweet seventeen-year-old charm.

"Tell her we said hi," Katy interrupted, "and will see her come basketball season."

"Yeah, looks like a good year. That coach really works them hard." Officer Norton walked towards his patrol car, and we all giggled.

"Orders ready." My dad bumped my elbow with his.

"This place hasn't changed much."

"Yeah, unlike everything else in this town."

"It's called progress Dad. Even Grandpa understood the need for progress."

"Are we talking about the same man? The same man who planted the same flowers in the same spot every year? The same man who bought his groceries from the same Mom & Pop store, even after the discount grocery stores moved in?"

"I think you're confusing the word progress. I remember one weekend I had come home from my first job in New York. I was debating on a writing assignment my boss wanted me to complete. I wasn't sure what to do, so naturally I went to visit Grandpa Frank..."

"Hello Elizabeth. How's life in the big city? I heard it has changed some since 1934."

"Yeah, I'd say the years between 1934 and 1994 have seen some changes in the Big Apple."

"Well, I'm sure you're doing just fine. Your father brings the newspaper articles you write to the house on Wednesday nights."

"Spaghetti nights."

"Yes, your Grandma still makes the best sauce, no lumps. Come Elizabeth, let me show you my flower garden."

"Everything looks beautiful as always. It must be nice to know exactly what you are going to do."

"What's this I hear in your voice? Do you want to trade the bright lights of New York for my boring life?"

"I'm just not sure if writing for the newspaper is where I want to end up."

"So, you are twenty-two and already know where you are going to spend your old age."

"I'll be twenty-three this July."

"Oh yes, you're practically an old lady. When you getting married?"

"Thanks Grandpa, I get that enough from the aunts."

"I know, but I couldn't resist. So, what's this about the newspaper boss?"

"I have this story to write about a political figure who has been linked to the wrong people, if you know what I mean."

"So, a politician with dirty hands, what's new?"

"Well, I actually believe he is a nice guy. Some of his projects have done a lot of good and I don't want to ignore that. My boss wants to sell papers, and that means giving readers something juicy to read."

"You're a writer Elizabeth. Turn the so-so good stuff into this juicy stuff your boss wants to read. I believe most people start off in the working world wanting to do good. Sometimes we meet so many not-so good people that we get tired and start to compromise. People start to say, 'well if I do this one bad thing it will let me do two good things, so I guess it's o.k.' Then, what do people remember? The one bad thing. You have to take care of all the little stuff, and that will bring you to the big stuff. It's like my flower garden, you see. I made sure I have good dirt. I give the flowers good fertilizer and maybe a little wine now and then. But what is it that I'm hoping for? Pretty flowers, yes? And you see the pretty flowers will come, if I take care of all the little things that need to be done. Sound good?"

"Sounds good. But, I know my boss will say 'Elizabeth, join the real world, keep up with the times, it's called progress.' I can just hear him now."

"Progress means moving forward to be a better person and to make things better for other people. Tell him that's exactly what you will write about Elizabeth. You will write about this man who is trying to make progress. Capisce?"

"Capisce."

"That was good advice from your Grandpa."

"Yeah, that article led to a few other exclusive interviews. They requested me, because they knew I would be honest and tell the whole story. Not just what sells."

"And a contact that helped give a start on publishing your first book. So you see, you should always do what's best, because you never know who is watching."

"Speaking of watching, how about the time?"

"It's a little after 1:00."

"Only a few more hours to prepare for my speech. I think I'm going to puke."

"Don't look at it as a speech. Just you talking about everything you learned from your grandfather and don't want to be forgotten."

"You make it sound so easy. Why don't you get up at the podium in church?"

"Not a chance." We walked back to his truck to drive home.

Upon returning home, I had to pass the kitchen to go upstairs to my room. As I passed the kitchen table, it was covered with food sent from friends in the neighborhood and family members. I saw one basket of fruit with some plums, my favorite. I decided to take it to my room. I walked upstairs and placed the basket beside my laptop. I glanced at the card. It read:

Dearest Marie,

I am so sorry to hear the news of Frank's passing. I know it has been a while since we spoke, but I want you to know you are welcome to come to Brooklyn anytime for a visit. I was thinking about all those crazy dreams your Frank and my Johnny had when we were younger. And who can forget the business. Marie, you are in our thoughts & prayers. We Love You- Johnny & Anna

"What business," I thought out loud.

"Are you talking to me dear?" My mom popped her head in the room.

"Umm, maybe. Look at this note mom. What does this mean, the business?"

"Oh yes. Your grandfather started a moving business in Brooklyn with a friend of his. I don't know much else."

"I don't believe this. Grandpa had his own business and he never told me. All those talks we had about me wanting to freelance and venture out on my own. He could have given me some better advice than just 'follow what makes you feel passion.' So Italian."

"Well, you'll just have to survive on the advice he gave you. No matter how Italian it sounds."

"I'm going to see Grandma Marie." I grabbed a plum, and yelled to my dad I was borrowing his truck.

"What about the eulogy?" shouted my mother from the top of the stairs.

"It's all in my head."

"That's what you said in the sixth grade when you had to write for an English class."

"Yeah so?"

"And you got a C plus that year."

"Shows what that teacher knew. I'm a published author," I shouted back sarcastically and ran out the door.

I hopped in the truck and drove to Grandma Marie's house. I started thinking to myself how now the house is just Grandma Marie's. It's not my grandparents' house anymore. I passed the railroad tracks and entered my grandparents' neighborhood. I pulled into the driveway and was happy to see my Grandma in the kitchen window. She was alone, thank goodness. I didn't feel like dealing with my aunts, and listening to their suggestions of what should be included in the eulogy. I walked inside and kissed her on the cheek.

"Hello Elizabeth. Did your mother send you to check on me? I finally convinced my sisters to go home. I have so much cleaning to do. Maybe you can help me wash the kitchen floor, yes? So many people have been over and it hasn't been washed in three days."

"No problem. And maybe while I mop, you can tell me about Grandpa's business with his friend Johnny?"

"Oh my. Now that's a story." Grandma Marie sat in a chair and supervised my floor washing.

"What do you mean the bill wasn't paid? Johnny said everything was set." Frank shouted on the phone to the insurance man. He finally gave up asking questions and slammed the phone down. "I don't believe this. Where is Johnny?"

"He's probably enjoying a nice dinner with Anna," replied Marie, as she sat down to eat supper. "Most newlyweds enjoy eating dinner together and talking to each other."

"Eat. How can I eat Marie, when I probably won't be able to work tomorrow? If the insurance says they never receive the money, then I cannot take the truck on the road. How am I supposed to have a moving business when I have no truck? Capisce?"

"I'm sure Johnny will have an answer. He is good with numbers. Come sit and eat, please Frank."

"No. I cannot enjoy my food with this up my head. I am going to see Johnny." Frank slammed the door and walked up the two flights of stairs to Johnny and Anna's apartment. "Johnny, are you home?"

"What is all that noise?" Johnny entered the hallway and encountered an angry Frank.

"What have you done with our insurance money? The man he call me and say I cannot drive truck tomorrow because we do not pay bill."

"Frank, relax," whispered Johnny. He walked toward Frank after closing his apartment door. "Listen, I'm a gonna pay that bill by the end of the week."

"End of the week. Today is Tuesday. We have three days with no work. That means three days with no money. We have customers Johnny. What are we gonna tell them?"

"I know, it's just I had some bills to pay and Anna and me-"

"No Anna. This is not Anna's fault. You promised no more gambling Johnny. You promised me and you promised Anna. This is America, Johnny. We both came here to make our dreams come true, yes? If you want to gamble and have no money, you could have stayed in Italy."

"Please Frank. Just give me to the end of the week. I promise after I pay off this guy, then you and me are going to have the best Brooklyn Movers business in the world."

"You do not know what you say. You do not know how to work for something. If you cannot work for you, then you work for your wife. She is going to have a baby, no? How are you going to be a good father if you make no money?"

"I will. We will. Frank, you always worry and then everything is o.k."

"It is o.k. because I make it o.k. Not this time. I do not fix this time."

"Oh my God. That sounds like a soap opera," I said to my Grandma Marie, as I mopped her kitchen floor. "What did you do?"

"We sold the trucks and paid the bills. There were more bills besides that one, and your Grandpa Frank was disgusted. We just paid everybody and closed the Brooklyn Movers business."

"Why didn't Grandpa just keep the business for himself?"

"We owed money and had to sell the trucks to pay the bills. And your Grandpa Frank thought it would be good to work with Johnny; maybe help him settle down and be good to Anna. Now that Johnny was not in the business, there was no reason to keep it."

"You must have been scared?"

"A little, but it also was a blessing. That time gave us a chance to ask what we really wanted our life to be. What our dreams were."

"Your passion. Grandpa's favorite word."

"Oh yes. He always said to live with passion and love, and then good things will come." Grandma Marie laughed and pointed to a spot on the floor that I missed.

"So, what did you do?"

"Well, a few days later I found out I was expecting. So, your Grandpa and I talked about how we wanted to raise our family. In Italy, we both grew up in neighborhoods where everybody visited each other and we had chickens in the backyard. We wanted that for our children, someplace safe. Not that Brooklyn wasn't safe in those days. We just wanted something different from New York."

"How on earth did you find little old Southington?"

"One day your Grandpa went to the bank to close an account and see if the business owed any more money. The banker thought highly of your Grandpa Frank for making sure everybody was paid and not being angry about what happened. At least he wasn't angry in public. This banker mentioned to your Grandpa that his brother worked in a town called Waterbury. The money was good and the town was very nice to raise a family. There was also a lot of Italians there, too."

"But you didn't live in Waterbury."

"I know, just listen and keep mopping. Now where was I...oh yes, so your Grandpa and I took the train one Saturday to see this Waterbury and we liked it very much. We decided to move there while we were waiting for the train back to Brooklyn. While we were waiting, this trolley stopped at the train station. Your Grandpa Frank thought it was so cute and wanted to ask the conductor more questions about this trolley. The trolley man lived in Southington, where they kept the trolleys overnight. And, they were looking for a man to grease the tracks. Well, the pay was good, but we never heard of this town called Southington. The man told your Grandpa that many Italians lived in the town, in a section called Goat's Island."

"Yeah, Goat's Island. So you came and bought a house just like that?"

"Well, your Grandpa came that Monday and saw this house and with a handshake and a loan from his new boss, the house was ours."

"You mean you didn't even see the house, Grandma?"

"No, but I know your Grandpa Frank and I trusted him completely. When you're married you have to, or it just doesn't work."

"But wait. What about Johnny and Anna? If you left mad at them, then why did she send you a fruit basket?"

"Who said we left mad? Anna and I always sent Christmas cards and they even came once to a Fourth of July party. Oh sure, at first your Grandpa was very upset and seemed like we were starting all over. Looking back, it's a good thing we got kicked in the ass."

"Oh, Grandma, you swore...I'm telling."

"Well, think about all the things that wouldn't have been if we stayed in Brooklyn. Sometimes you need to meet the people who kick and knock you down. If you never meet them, you'll never meet the people who help you back up."

"So, here you are."

"Here we are. Your Grandpa and I followed our hearts, did what we thought was right and felt good about. That, Elizabeth, is the secret to life," winked my Grandma Marie. "These floors look spotless. Thank you Elizabeth. Grab a piece of candy on your way out."

"Are you kicking me out?"

"Don't you have a eulogy to write?"

I returned home knowing exactly what I wanted to say and how to say it. As I passed my mother on the way upstairs, she gave me the same worried look that my editor does when I'm closing in on a deadline. When I write, I can't think about the time or the deadline. I just have to be ready to write and then everything just pours onto my laptop. This was the time. I sat down in my chair and started to write the welcoming to all who will be in attendance at the church. I paused for a moment and reflected on how I will be feeling that day. Standing in front of all those people. Standing in front of my grandfather's casket.

"Whatcha doing?" asked my cousin Johnny as he peeked into my room.

"Oh my God. You scared me Johnny."

"You wouldn't make a very good soldier," he laughed, as he dusted off his new Sergeant stripes on his arm.

"Very nice. Sergeant First Class. Does this mean you don't need food stamps anymore?"

"Tell me about it. Protecting my country and I can barely pay my bills."

"Welcome to my world."

"What do you mean, a successful writer like you? I thought we were having the dinner after the funeral at your mansion?"

"No, and right now I'm just hoping I make it to the dinner. I started writing the eulogy and then I got to thinking about standing in front of everybody and the casket."

"Oh yeah, caskets freak you out. That has nothing to do with that night?"

"It has everything to do with that night." I quickly interrupted.

"I don't know if this is such a great idea." Tommy shook nervously in his Winnie-the-Pooh pajamas.

"Oh, it won't be that bad," I replied, in my confident ten-year old voice.

"Shhh. You guys are going to scare away all the spirits," whispered Johnny. He held his Star Wars saber sword in front of the three of us for protection.

"Where is the casket you told us about?" I whispered.

"Just follow me. And no talking." Johnny answered.

We slowly crept over a small hill and could hear the river in the near distance. I looked behind me and realized we could no longer see Johnny's house. Whenever I slept over Johnny's house, I would look out the window and watch the cemetery at night. I'd wonder if any spirits were roaming the graves. Now, Johnny had volunteered to be my personal guide on this summer evening in 1981.

"I see it. It's right over here." Johnny pointed to something with his saber sword.

"I think it's empty," I responded, as we approached the metal box.

"Of course it's empty. The person rose from the dead. Everybody who dies gets to rise from the dead. If you don't, then that means you burn in hell."

"That's not true. I don't see any burning bodies." Tommy's voice was shaky.

"Oh yeah, then what about all that steam we see rising from the graves? That's the bodies burning you moron. That's why people aren't allowed in the cemetery at night, because that's when God decides who gets burned. They scream and moan while their bodies are on fire."

"Stop it Johnny! You are scaring him."

"Well, that's the way it is. Why do you think the cemetery never runs out of room to bury the bodies, huh? It's because the funeral guys come back in a few days and dig up everything. If the casket is empty, they know the person went to heaven. If the casket has black ashes in it, they know they are in hell. That's why those funeral guys always wear black. It hides all the ashes they get on their clothes."

"You can't prove that."

"Shh, Elizabeth. Not so loud. I hear something." Johnny pushed Tommy and me to the ground.

"It's just a car," said Tommy.

"It's Satan's car," answered Johnny.

"Satan doesn't have a car," whispered Tommy.

"Of course he does. Don't you listen in church? The priest always says if you're not good you will be driven to the depths of hell."

"I hope it's not here for us."

"We have to make a run for it. It looks like Satan has already started his fire and will be coming out any time to burn some bodies, so they can live in damnation forever."

"How do you know that?"

75

"Look, Elizabeth, the windows are getting all smoky."

"I hear moaning," interrupted Tommy.

"That's the chants. Satan is calling all those who are impure and have to live an eternity in hell."

"Well, I ain't picking up the phone!" I quickly ran towards the river. Suddenly, I felt my feet lose control. I tripped, rolled a bit, and then stopped with a sudden thud. I looked up and realized I had landed in a cement box. Johnny and Tommy were both staring at me from above.

"Well, aren't you the smarty pants. You're just giving Satan an invitation to take you now," smirked Johnny.

"Just help me out. This is way too freaky."

"You're the one who wanted to see the spirits."

"Well, we didn't see any spirits Johnny, so there." Tommy answered back with his hands on his hip.

"How do you know? You were too busy running away from Satan to check him out. I happened to see him with my own two eyes."

"You did?" I brushed myself off.

"Yeah, and he wasn't happy that people were spying on him either. It's a good thing he took off, or he would have seen Elizabeth in this casket and thought she was a soul waiting to be burned."

"Elizabeth isn't going to burn," answered Tommy. "What did she ever do that was so bad?"

"Satan always takes the souls of children. Everybody knows that, stupid."

"I hear voices over here."

"Who said that?"

"Not me," Tommy and I answered in unison.

"It was me." Uncle Joe approached with a flashlight.

"Dad, what are you doing here?" asked Johnny.

"What are you doing here? Your mothers are going to have a fit. You're outside, in a cemetery and walking around in your pajamas. Look at you Tommy. Your pajamas have dirt on them."

"No Uncle Joseph. It is ashes."

"Well, whatever you have on you, your mother isn't going to be happy. So, did you see any ghosts, Elizabeth?"

"No, but Johnny saw Satan. He got really mad and ran away."

"Yeah," interrupted Johnny. "But if you want to see him Dad, he took off over that way. He's wearing Fruit of the Loom underwear."

"Ha-Ha." Johnny and I both laughed, as we remembered our first encounter with 'Satan'.

"That poor guy. Just trying to get laid, and had a bunch of kids interrupting his romantic evening."

"Yeah, real romantic. Having sex in a cemetery."

"Well, I better let you write this eulogy. It's almost dinner time, and who knows how long we'll be stuck at the table."

"Gee, thanks for reminding me. Maybe I'll ask my mom to just make me a plate of something and I'll eat up here."

"Sounds like a good idea."

I quickly began to type all the thoughts and memories about Grandpa Frank that were entering my head. Before I knew it, the cuckoo clock was announcing the time of five o'clock.

'Fantastico!' I said to myself as I clicked print on my laptop.

"You say something dear?" My mother peeked into my room.

"I just finished the eulogy for Grandpa and it ain't that bad if I do say so myself."

"Just in time to forget about it for a while, and enjoy dinner with the family."

"Isn't that an oxymoron, mom?"

"Put on something nice and wear a smile."

"Hey mom, are you happy?"

"Happy? I'm too busy to stop and think if I'm happy. That's the problem with you kids...too much time to sit under a tree and ask if you're happy."

I printed out the eulogy and read it a few times to myself. I was pleased with my work and believed I couldn't add or delete anything more. Once I can say that about my writings, I know it's complete and I send it to the editor. This time however, there was no editor to send it to...just me, myself and I. Tomorrow was the wake and the next day was the funeral. So, that gave me one good night sleep tonight, and I decided to do just that. Before I could put on my pajamas though, I had to eat dinner with my family; extended cousins and all. I changed my blouse and put on a pair of Dockers. I figured I'd be wearing a skirt and dress the next two days, so tonight I should be comfortable. I looked in the mirror, fixed my hair a bit, and decided that was the best I was going to get. I placed the eulogy in an envelope and hid it under my laptop. Now, all I had to do was survive another family dinner.

"Hi Elizabeth," said my cousin Laura. Laura is my Aunt Mary's daughter. She lives in Southington with her husband and three kids.

"Hi. How's the world been treating you?"

"Not bad. The kids are all in school, so I have some quiet time during the day before they arrive home to destroy the house."

"I don't think I ever saw your house...in person at least. I see it once a year on your Christmas card though."

"Oh, aren't those cards great. When I first saw the house I knew it would look fabulous for the holidays."

"So, that was your main reason for buying the house?"

"No silly, I mean don't get me wrong, the house is a beautiful house, but we also love the town, too."

"Really, do you volunteer at any community organizations?"

"Well, no."

"Oh, well you must volunteer at the school a lot."

"Umm, during the holiday season I help with the parties. The kids are so cute when they are dressed up."

"And the kids who are having difficulty in school, you must have a program that volunteers can sign-up and help them right?"

"I'm not sure. You know the kids keep me busy and before you know it, it's dinner time."

"Right, kids love to eat. There must be a lot of kids in your neighborhood. All those homes with so many bedrooms, one would think so?"

"We don't really see our neighbors too much. You know, everyone is so busy working."

"I see, so you bought the house because?"

"Hey, are you going to write about this in one of your articles?" Laura asked with a smile.

"No, people in Manhattan are tired of hearing about the 'problems' suburban mothers have. But maybe I'll write an article on how neighborhoods have changed throughout the years."

"Well, Southington still has all those qualities. That's why we are raising our kids here." Laura lifted her wine glass.

"You don't say." I walked away with a deviled egg in my hand.

"Are you starting trouble?" My sister motioned to sit down next to her and my niece for dinner.

"Who me? I'm just asking questions."

"That's usually how you get in trouble."

"Where's your hubby?"

"He's somewhere with Dad, I guess."

"How's my favorite niece?" I asked while pinching her cheeks.

"She's been a great helper to mommy getting the baby room ready, right?"

"Are you prepared?"

"Yeah, we are just a little squished. I would like something a little bigger, but we love the neighborhood."

"Oh, you know your neighbors?"

"Of course, why wouldn't I?"

"You should talk to our cousin Laura. She bought their house because of all the benefits, but right now she can only think of one."

"Well, we love our little house. Even if it's not on the better side of town."

"Just what is the better side of town?"

"You know where the swamp was?"

"You gotta be kidding me."

"Nope, people just saw these nice houses and bought, bought, bought."

"I can't wait to get a Christmas card from Laura in ten years."

"What?"

"Nothing. The swamp... I remember when we would all meet up there in the summer time and spend the whole day just playing."

"Yeah, and trespassing."

"Kids don't trespass, they explore." I laughed, as I started to recall a hot July day in 1980. I was just about to turn nine years old...

"This is gonna be perfect," said Nick.

"I think we should get a tarp for the roof, too," added Johnny. "That way, we can even come here when it rains."

"Yeah cool," the rest of the gang said, which included Joe Jr, Laura, Beth, Katherine, Tommy, my sister and me.

"Yeah, and this club is for blood only." said Nick.

"Knock it off with the blood stuff," said Beth. "Let's just finish the roof today. My dad said it's gonna rain tomorrow, so all our work on the inside will be ruined."

"Little Miss Practical," her brother Tommy replied, as he put his hands on his hips and swung about.

"Oh shut up." Katherine pushed her brother in a mud puddle and started walking up the hill.

"Hey, you got my jeans all wet."

"Who's being practical now? Come on, didn't you guys say we needed a tarp?"

"Yeah, you got one?" asked Joe Jr.

"Of course not, but I know where to get one. Look over there."

"You gotta be a freakin' lunatic." said Nick.

"Isn't that Mr. O'Langley's place? And how are we gonna get that tarp off his barn roof?" asked my sister, Rose.

"Easy. The boys can climb on the roof and throw it to us girls waiting on the ground."

"Why are you girls waiting on the ground?" asked Tommy.

"Because it was my plan, and I'm a girl, so what I say goes."

"Oh who cares. I still don't think we can get that tarp without crazy O'Langley seeing us," said Nick.

"He's not crazy," I answered.

"Is, too. He's Irish ain't he? And Grandpa says all Irish people are crazy."

"Irish people aren't crazy," interrupted Laura, "they just drink all day."

"Grandpa drinks, and he isn't crazy," I said.

"Grandpa only drinks on Sunday with the Lord," snapped back Nick.

"Alright, are we doing this or what?" Katherine started to walk towards O'Langley's barn.

"I'm no chicken." Nick joined her and we all proceeded to follow behind them.

"I think he is in the house eating lunch," said Beth.

"Yeah, when are we eating our lunch?" asked Tommy.

"After you get the tarp off the roof."

"Shhh. We have to be as quiet as possible," said Nick. "The last thing I want is a crazy, Irish drunk man chasing me in the woods."

"Come on guys, we can hop on this roof and stretch to pull down the tarp." Johnny hopped onto the roof covering the pigpen.

"I think this is gonna work," said Nick, as we were all able to hop on the lower roof and pull the tarp down.

"Everybody find an end and start bunching it towards the middle," ordered Katherine.

"What's gonna happen to Mr. O'Langley's barn when it rains tomorrow," I asked.

"Oh, his barn will be fine. He doesn't use it anymore for animals. All he's got left are these pigs," answered Johnny.

"Besides, we can bring it back at the end of the summer when we tear down the fort," said Laura.

"Tear down the fort?" questioned Nick and Johnny. "After you made us steal...I mean borrow this tarp. We're gonna do what?"

"I heard my dad saying that somebody is gonna buy all this land. We probably won't be able to come back here next year. Besides, next summer Katherine and I will be going to band practice all summer. And Johnny, you said you were going to baseball camp next year."

"Yeah, I guess this is our last summer together."

"Why don't we sleep in the fort tonight and then we can return the tarp in the morning?"

"Great idea, Elizabeth. We can stay up all night if we want."

"Everyone return here at 9:30 tonight and bring a flashlight."

We all went our separate ways home on our bikes. My sister and I decided to stop at the park and eat our lunch by the pond. It was there, that we saw Mr. and Mrs. Nuccio walking in the park.

"Hello Mr. & Mrs. Nuccio," my sister and I said in unison.

"Hello girls," said Mr. Nuccio.

"What are you two ladies doing here?" asked Mrs. Nuccio.

"We were just eating our lunch before we rode our bikes the rest of the way home," my sister answered.

"Well, it's a great day for a picnic," replied Mrs. Nuccio.

"Yeah. Any day is a great day when there is no school." I replied.

"We better get going on our bikes, Elizabeth."

"Are you sure you girls don't want us to drive you home?" asked Mr.Nuccio.

"No thanks." We packed up our things and jumped on our bikes.

"That was close," said my sister, as we cruised down the hill on our banana seat bikes.

"What are you talking about?"

"You might of slipped and told them what we were going to do tonight."

"I would not have slipped."

"Oh, it doesn't matter now...we got away. Now we have to figure out how to get out of the house tonight."

"The front door sounds good to me."

We pedaled up Green Mountain Drive and put our bikes in the garage. We shouted to our mother we were home thru the kitchen window. She told us to put on our bathing suits. She would be out in a few minutes. My sister and I ran to our clubhouse and changed into our bathing suits. We waited on the deck for our mother and, once we saw her come out the back door, did a cannon ball into the pool. My sister and I discussed our escape plan in between splashes, as our mother read her McCall's magazine. Everything was going perfectly.

"Keep quiet until we are on the bikes," my sister whispered as we crept down the stairs. It was exactly nine o'clock and the moon was bright enough to help us find our bikes without turning on our flashlights. We hopped on our bikes and pedaled down our road and turned left instead of right. We decided to meet up with Laura, Beth, Katherine and Tommy. We figured there was safety in numbers.

"Hey guys, you made it." My sister waved, as we saw them approaching our way.

"Awesome. That was so easy." said my cousin Tommy.

"Let's keep going," said Laura, "we don't want anyone to see us."

We arrived at the fort and saw Johnny, Joe Jr. and Nick fixing the tarp on the roof. It looks like they also started a small fire, too.

"Hey, this looks great," said Beth. We all got off our bikes and sat around the fire.

"I could live out here forever," said Joe Jr. with a smile.

"Wait till it starts to rain," answered back Johnny.

"Is it gonna rain tonight?" asked Katherine.

"It doesn't look like rain," answered Johnny.

"Let's make the s'mores," said Nick.

"Hey, look at all those lights!" exclaimed Rose.

"Those are fire engines," I said.

"Yep, there must be a fire somewhere," said Tommy, as he looked around the hill.

"It's us stupid," said Johnny. He smacked Tommy on the back of the head. That cranky old Mr. O'Langley called the firemen."

"Oh no, we are going to be arrested," Laura said nervously.

"Oh please, they can't arrest kids. We aren't doing anything wrong," shouted Johnny, as he motioned to everyone to sit down. "Just stay calm."

"Hello kids," said the fire chief as he approached our fort. "Nice night for camping, isn't it?"

"Oh, we're not camping, sir," said Johnny. "We are exploring."

"Exploring," responded the fire chief with a smirk on his face. "Well, that's a little different. You see I was told someone was trespassing on Mr. O'Langley's property and they started a fire in the woods."

"What's trespassing?" Tommy asked.

"It's when you are somewhere that you don't belong," the chief answered.

"We are explorers," said Joe Jr. confidently. "We travel to unknown places and do no harm."

"Is that so? Well now, I think that sounds like a great job. Tell me, will this job have you home by 11:00 o'clock?"

"Absolutely," answered a wise Laura. "And we'll make sure the fire is put out too."

"After we eat the s'mores," interrupted Tommy. "I am hungry."

"Of course," answered the fire chief, as he waved goodbye and walked down the hill.

"Well, who's up there?" asked Mr. O'Langley.

"Just some future politicians. They'll be gone in about thirty minutes. Just take a walk up there after they leave to make sure the camp fire is completely out."

"And what about my property."

"It's a swamp, Charlie. You're lucky you found some out-of-towner to buy it."

84

"I can't believe we got away with that," I said to my sister, as we finished our dinner.

"Yeah, sometimes I drive by there and look at those homes. If those people only knew."

"Do you think Mom and Dad knew what we did?"

"Of course," said my Dad as he snuck up behind us. "Your Grandma Marie is looking for you. I think she is in the kitchen."

"Where else would she be." I got up from my chair. "I think I'll just go for a walk and then turn in."

"This town isn't as safe as it was when you were nine years old."

"Thanks for the reminder, Dad." I kissed him goodnight and went into the kitchen.

"Oh, Elizabeth, I'm glad I saw you before I left. I want to show you something." My Grandma Marie took my hand and we walked outside. She reached into the backseat of my Uncle's car and pulled out an envelope. "This is a letter written by your grandpa's mother before we left Italy. I would like to read it to you."

"That's amazing, I would love to hear it Grandma." We both sat down on the back steps.

"My Dearest Francesco, I send with you all my love as you sail to the Americas. I am happy you go with a wife. Take care of each other and be careful. I know you will make me proud. I will be far away from you, but I think of you always. You will always be my little boy and I love you always. Love, your Momma."

"Grandpa kept that letter all this time?"

"Yes. I wanted you to have this. You keep it safe. I wanted you to know that your Grandpa Frank was someone's little boy. He was more than just a Grandpa, capisce?"

"Capisce," I answered and kissed my Grandma goodnight. I placed the letter in my pocket and walked down the driveway.

The sky was so clear and it was a great night for a walk. I had a certain destination in mind, too. My folks lived less than a mile from the cemetery, and that was where my feet led me. I walked through the front gates and thought how I would have never done this a few years ago. I never liked funerals and seeing dead people. I still don't, but I've learned to accept it more. During the war, I had to attend a lot of funerals of former service buddies. In the beginning, I felt guilty because they stayed in the service and I didn't. I was alive and living a great life, and theirs had ended by the time they were thirty. I guess it made me more of a risk taker, because I started to realize failing wasn't as bad as never trying; never knowing what might be. Sometimes, I wished I had that confidence in my early twenties. I know my Grandpa and Grandma had it. They came to America with nothing but faith. Lately, I understand my Grandpa Frank's advice more and more. Maybe that's why I'm in this cemetery tonight. I wanted to see his final resting place before anyone else did. It's just a piece of land, but when a loved one is there, it becomes a sanctuary to those the person left behind. My Grandpa Frank never had a spot to come and visit his parents; just his letter. Maybe he was luckier than me. He could carry that letter with him wherever he traveled, and feel his mother's love. In a few days, I would be back in New York and have no sanctuary to visit. I started to feel more relaxed about the wake tomorrow. I would actually have time to visit my Grandpa Frank. See him one last time, share stories with my cousins, and maybe laugh a little too. Yes, I thought, as I approached the stone with Grandpa Franks name on it. He would have wanted us to share a few stories and laugh. 'Okay, Grandpa Frank, that's what I'll do', I said out loud. 'I hope you like the eulogy...wherever you are.'

The Wake

It's always amazing how many people attend wakes. I guess you never realize how many lives one person affects, until they die. My Grandpa Frank lived in Southington for much of his life. I just assumed most of his friends had passed. As I walked into the funeral parlor, I could see the many flowers surrounding his casket and other arrangements decorating the wall to the side of his casket. Grandpa Frank looked like he was sleeping peacefully, as if he was taking a nap after enjoying a nice glass of his homemade wine. I stopped to admire the flowers and read the cards. My Grandma Marie approached and joined me in this endeavor. She had a story to tell after I read each signature. I listened patiently as I held her shaky hand. From the corner of my eye, I could see some guests starting to make a line to pay their respects.

"Grandma, maybe we should sit down for a bit and let these people visit Grandpa." I motioned with my hand to the line that was forming at the entranceway.

"Do we have guests already?"

"The man in front looks familiar to me."

"Well, I better little Elizabeth! After all that candy I gave you."

"Mr. Ferrucci?" Grandma and I walked towards Grandpa's faithful friend.

"If anyone would be first in line to see Frank, it would be you." Grandma smiled and kissed Mr. Ferrucci on the cheek.

"Such a good man, Marie.....such a good man." Mr. Ferrucci's eyes began to water.

"Come and see all the flowers," Grandma instructed. She took his hand and I was left to find my parents sitting patiently in the parlor.

"Who is that?" asked my sister, as I joined my immediate family about two rows away from the casket.

"That's Mr. Ferrucci."

"He got old."

"It happens to the best of us," joked my father, as he turned around and looked at my sister and me. "How you holding up?"

"I'm fine."

"I meant your sister. You know she's pregnant."

"Oh sure, forget the single, non-pregnant people. After all, all we do is work every day and contribute to your social security."

"Thank you very much."

"I'm fine," answered Rose.

"Oh boy, look who's coming this way," I whispered to my sister.

"Well, at least it's just Aunt Sophia. I don't see the other two."

"Just wait."

"Hello girls," said Aunt Sophia, as she sat in the chair next to me. "Tell me, how is your Grandma doing?"

"I think she is doing just fine. She seems to be chatting up a storm with Mr. Ferrucci over there."

"Yes, such a nice man. I miss seeing his store downtown. Today, there is no more shopping downtown. These kids don't know what it is to live in a nice small town, right Vincent?"

"Yes, the town has changed. Too many people moved in and now I don't know half the people that live here."

"Maybe Frank had the right idea. He made his garden his own special place, and all the old friends would sit with him under his grapevine. He really enjoyed his retirement years. Just talking with friends and bragging about his grandchildren of course," smiled Aunt Sophia.

"That conversation must have been about me," interrupted my cousin Johnny, who was dressed in his Class B Army uniform.

"Where are all the shiny medals?"

"I'm saving that for tomorrow, Elizabeth." Johnny pulled up a chair and joined our little circle. "Sure are a lot of people, huh?"

"Yeah, but a lot of people come to the wake. There probably won't be this many people at the funeral tomorrow."

"No, just the reporter from the town newspaper."

"What?"

"Oh yes," interrupted Aunt Sophia, "I called my friend Sylvia whose grandson works at the newspaper here in town. I told her my sister's famous granddaughter was giving the eulogy. I invited him to the house after the funeral tomorrow, too. He wants to talk to you. I thought it would help you get some publicity, yes?"

"Thanks, Aunt Sophia." I glared at my cousin Johnny.

"Oh, you'll be fine. Let's get some coffee in the other room. I have a feeling we're going to be here a while."

"I can't believe she invited a reporter to Grandpa Frank's funeral."

"Oh, he would have been there anyway. The guy knew Grandpa Frank."

"What do you mean?"

"The guy does some stories every so often on local people who have some interesting stories about the town. Didn't your folks ever tell you?"

"No. What did Grandpa Frank talk about?"

"Just the good old days. What the town was like, and how everybody knew everybody else. And of course, he talked about his grapevine and how the grapes tasted just like the ones in Italy. I always wondered why he never went back to Italy. Even just to visit."

"I do." My thoughts took me back to Christmas Eve in 1988.

"Merry Christmas." I kissed Grandpa Frank's cheek and tried to balance the cookie platter with one hand.

"Merry Christmas, Elizabeth. You are getting big, a senior in high school. Any news about college, yet?"

"Not yet, but I've thought of some other options too." I gave him a look with my eyes as if to say 'follow me.'

"Yes, let me help you with that tray." We walked through the kitchen and into the parlor. We sat on the couch covered with plastic.

"I have a really great idea, but I'm not sure what my parents might say."

"If it is a great idea, how can you go wrong, yes?"

"Yeah, but I'll be going far from home."

"Sometimes, that is a good thing. When you are away from home, you realize how close you always are to the ones you love, capisce?"

"No...not quite."

"Look at me and your Grandma. We are so far from home, but we remember all the people we love in Italy and we live a good life here in America, yes?"

"Yeah."

"Well, why do you think we choose to live this way? We remember everything our parents taught us and we want to make them proud. Grandma and me remember what made us happy when we were children, a long time ago. We want the same for our children. And now, your parents want the same from you. But it all began from somewhere far away. Capisce now, Elizabeth?"

"Yes, I get what you're trying to say. I just wish someone would tell me what is the best choice."

"There is never a best choice. You just make a choice and then make the best of it."

"Easier said than done."

"Don't tell me about easy."

"I know," I interrupted, "the boat sailing across the ocean with no food."

"A boat, I think it was a canoe."

"Oh, come on now."

"I can still see my parents waving goodbye." Grandpa Frank became quiet with a faraway look in his eye.

"It must be hard this time of year without your parents. And you never went back to see them."

"I see them every time I look in my children's eyes and my grandchildren's eyes. I know I make them proud when I see all my grandchildren graduate from high school. Now, they go to college. No high school diploma for me. But in so little time, my grandchildren go to college like the Rockefellers. I say, only in America."

"I do plan on going to college, but I want to travel a bit, too. I've never been anywhere and I want to see the country."

"Travel is as good as any education, Elizabeth. You learn so much from other people and you learn to respect people from all parts of the world. Yes, travel is a good idea. You send me lots of postcards?"

"Yes, of course. I just have to finish basic training first."

"So, you will be wearing boots during this traveling?"

"Traveling and getting paid. I'll be working for the Stars & Stripes and stationed out west for a while."

"Ahh, you say hi to Roy Rogers for me."

"Maybe you can come visit me?"

"Maybe you can come home once in a while. We will sit under my grapevine, on a nice summer evening, and you can tell me all about the wild, wild west."

"I don't think it's the wild west anymore Grandpa."

"Good, then your mother won't have anything to worry about when you tell her." We walked back to the kitchen to pour a glass of wine.

"I remember that Christmas Eve," said Johnny, as I finished my cup of coffee.

"We actually finished our job training at the same time out in California."

"Yeah, California was great. And it was nice hanging out with all our friends before some left for the war."

"I wonder where they are now?"

"I bet most of them aren't wearing a uniform."

"I bet you're right. I guess I was always too scared to join the civilian world."

"It's just as crazy as military life. You aren't missing much."

"I know I have better stories than you do from your posh job in Manhattan."

"I'll second that. Sometimes I tell stories at work about the things that happened in basic training, and nobody believes me. Swear."

"Swear? You swear?" Johnny said with a grin. "That's why you got guard duty one night, right?"

"Something like that. Oh yes, I remember it well."

"All right, this ain't the girl scouts. Let's move it up this hill and now." The Drill Sergeant shouted in the hot afternoon South Carolina sun.

"I don't think I can make it Manciano," said Private Rochette,

"Sure you can." We marched along with our backpacks and rifles adding the extra pounds.

"This Drill Sergeant is whacked," added Private O'Conal in third squad, while wiping the sweat from the back of her neck.

"We'll be home soon."

"I don't see the barracks at all," Rochette answered.

"Not that home. I mean home-home. You know, real food and people actually take a car to get somewhere."

"A car, what's that?" O'Conal was the one person I could count on to try to make the other girls laugh. We were bunk buddies and always had each other's back. We were both from Connecticut. She enlisted in the Army to help pay for college, just like me.

"What's so funny soldiers?" screamed the Drill Sergeant, from the middle of the platoon.

"Soldiers...you see soldiers," smirked O'Conal. "I see a bunch of girls in need of showers and a night out with some men."

"Shh!" answered Rochette, "he's coming this way."

"Sorry to interrupt the conversation ladies. But the rest of us are trying to march and be all we can be. After all, it's a great day to be in the Army!"

"Yes Drill Sergeant. It is a great day to be in the Army."

"What about you Rochette? Is it a great day to be in the Army?" asked the Drill Sergeant.

"Well, I'm really not quite-"

"Who do you think you're talking to?" The Drill Sergeant's spit was flying everywhere. "Do I look like your mother? You've got to be a f-in' idiot!"

"There really is no reason to swear, Drill Sergeant," I interrupted. "You know a little verbal praise goes a lot farther than-"

"Two f-in' idiots!"

"Hey, all this talk is making me miss my boyfriend," smirked O'Conal. She smacked Rochette on the back, and the rest of the platoon started to laugh.

"Well, I guess we just aren't tired enough. We have all this energy to think about our boyfriends. How about taking the long way back to the barracks, Manciano?"

"I think that's a great idea, Drill Sergeant. After all, it's a great day to be in the Army." I started to sing cadence to the platoon. We marched passed the rifle range and checked out all the guys shooting that day.

"Hey Manciano, there's your Malone."

"Hey Anderson, start singing Mighty, Mighty Alpha." That was the signal Malone and I used to let each other know when one of us had guard duty that night.

"We don't have guard duty tonight," O'Conal said to me.

"We will when the Drill Sergeant finds out we lost another guard vest."

"Oh shit."

"Ain't that the truth." O'Conal dropped it down the port-o-potty while we were at the range this morning.

"Here comes the moment of truth." I said out loud, as we approached an intersection.

"Where the hell is your guard vest?" screamed the Drill Sergeant.

"Again, Drill Sergeant, we really need to discuss all this swearing. You know educated people don't feel-"

"I feel like stapling a guard vest to your buddy's chest. The two of you will find that guard vest. And until you do, you will have guard duty every night. You understand soldiers."

"Yes, Drill Sergeant." O'Conal and I ran to the back of the platoon and returned to the formation.

"So, you got your guard duty Manciano. But I didn't want it every night."

"We won't have it every night. You're getting that vest back tonight."

"Oh shit."

"Again with the swearing. Where do you think we are?"

"We are two Yankees in a place where they serve grits for breakfast. I think a little swearing is the least of your problems."

That night we signed in for guard duty at our usual 0100 hours. We had two hours to get to the range, retrieve the guard vest and return back to the barracks by 0300 hours. We decided to enlist our partners in crime- my boyfriend, Malone and his bunk buddy- Cole. Their barracks were just across the street. After getting them up-to-date on our predicament, they agreed to join the mission.

"The port-o-potty is over here," O'Conal whispered, as the pine trees swayed in the Carolina moonlight.

"Thank God there's a full moon tonight," said Cole.

"Maybe that's why the Drill Sergeants were so crazy today," answered Malone.

"They're crazy every day." I opened the door to the port-o-potty.

We surveyed the problem with our flashlights. The port-o-potties were all stationed on top of one big tank. We could smell the chemicals dumped below to try to eliminate the smell of crap on those hot Carolina days. The military port-o-potties weren't your basic civilian style crap boxes. Uncle Sam had furnished us with a small room that had a circle of holes to sit and 'do your business.' It wasn't very private, but it served the purpose. The retrieval of the vest was just a matter of lifting the cover of the port-o-potty holes, lowering a body into the tank and grabbing the vest; which was clearly visible from where we were standing. Its bright orange color was smeared a bit with crap, but the fluorescent strips made it easy to find.

"Well, which one of you ladies is taking the plunge?" asked Malone.

"O'Conal," I answered. "After all, you're the reason we're here."

"Great. What about your responsibility as the platoon guide?"

"Hold your breath." I began to grab her ankles.

"Wait. Wait. I don't think my asthma is going to agree with this."

"You can't have asthma and be in the military," said Malone.

"Well, it's only activated when I'm dumped in shit boxes."

"We are running out of time," I said. "Just give me your flashlight and stand back."

"I promise I won't let go," said Malone. He and Cole lowered my body down the hole.

"Move me to the left a little."

"Do you have it?" asked O'Conal.

"I got it." My eyes began to tear from all the chemicals and waste.

"Thank God they didn't drop you," said O'Conal. I was brought to the surface and staggered outside to breathe the clean air.

"Don't look so relieved. You're the one that has to wear this tomorrow. Just another great day to be in the Army."

"Oh, those were some fun times."

"Yeah, fun memories. I'm sure you wouldn't want to do that again."

"Not on your life."

"Excuse me," interrupted the funeral director. "Your Grandmother would like you to say a prayer as we end the wake services this evening, Elizabeth."

"Oh, umm, okay. I'll be right there." My heart skipped a beat as I walked back into the room and saw my Grandpa Frank. As I approached the front to greet the priest, voices began to cease. I took a deep breath and waited for the priest to say his part. I figured he would give me a sign when it was my turn to speak.

"Thank you everyone for coming to console our dear friend, Marie, during her time of grief. I know Frank is smiling at us while he witnesses all the warm and caring people who chose to be here with Marie and offer their support during these difficult days that come with losing a loved one. I have the honor of introducing one of Frank's granddaughters, Elizabeth, who would like to end our time here tonight with a prayer. Elizabeth."

"Thank you Father. I think I speak for my Grandma Marie and all the family when I say thank you to all of Grandpa Frank's friends and members of the community who paid their respects tonight. Your warm words about my Grandpa Frank where a great comfort and it's nice to know such a quiet man made such a great impact on so many people. Now, let's bow our heads and say the Lord's Prayer together."

"Nice job, Elizabeth."

"Thanks, Dad. I think that was a good idea to help me prepare for tomorrow's big event."

"Just remember, it's all family," responded my mother.

"My worst critics." I remembered the response I received from my first published book.

"So what do you think, mom?"

"I don't think you should have used all those swear words."

"Well, drunks swear, and I was writing about a drunk."

"Your Grandma thinks it cost too much money."

"There's always the library. Anything else wrong with the book?"

"No, but I haven't seen the aunts yet either."

"Oh brother, I forgot they could read."

"That's not nice."

"They're not nice. At least they'll have something to talk about at the beauty parlor. Well, I better go. Max is coming over and we're going to the park with Steinbeck."

"I could never understand why people have dogs in the city."

"I bet Steinbeck gets more exercise than some suburban dogs do, mom."

"Well, I'll let you go then. I'll call you during the week. Bye."

"Bye, mom." I grabbed Steinbeck's leash, which always gets a hyper response from him. I walked to the lobby and saw Max talking to the doorman.

"Perfect timing." I approached Max and the doorman, Charlie.

"I was just coming up," said Max.

"Yeah, Yeah. Let's go, Steinbeck is anxious to get to the park."

"Me,too." Max swung the strap of his camera case over his shoulder.

"Taking pictures today?"

"I need some shots of happy people in New York City. It's for a tourist magazine."

"Sounds like fun."

"It's paying the bills."

"And what would you rather be doing?"

"Traveling the country and taking pictures of Americana."

"So do it."

"I've been thinking about it. My family would think I'm nuts."

"If they're like my family, they probably already do. But, do you see me worrying about my family?"

"They didn't like the book?"

"I don't think it's a matter of not liking the book. I just think it's in their nature to critique everything. In a loving way, of course."

"What about your Grandpa Frank?"

"I haven't heard from him yet, but it takes him longer to read."

"I haven't seen him in a while. I'd love to take his picture."

"He doesn't like doing those formal pictures, but you could ask."

"I wasn't thinking of something formal. Just him in everyday life. That's what I want to create a book about. People living in everyday America."

"If you want, we can take a drive to Connecticut next weekend. My town has a festival in the fall, and I haven't been to it in a while."

"If there's food, I'm in."

Max and I arrived in my hometown the following weekend. The fall colors were in full bloom. I loved this time of year in New England. We pulled into my grandparent's driveway around 11:30, just in time to walk with my grandparents to the festival for lunch.

"Marie, Elizabeth is here." Grandpa Frank opened the screen door and welcomed us inside.

"Let me get the first kiss." Grandma Marie lovingly pushed aside my Grandpa Frank.

"How are you Max?"

"Very well, Grandpa Frank."

"Well, let's walk downtown. That will give my kitchen floor time to dry."

"Oh yes, your Grandma has been busy cleaning for your visit."

"Oh, I hope you didn't go to too much trouble," responded Max. "We'll only be staying overnight."

"My wife loves to clean. And, having young people in the house is always a good thing."

"Alright then. Let's check out this festival Elizabeth keeps bragging about."

The fair was a great way for Grandpa Frank to discuss his life story with Max. I think someone wanting to find out what America was all about from an immigrant amused my Grandpa. We showed Max the downtown, and Grandpa retold stories about how it used to look and all the 'old-timers' that owned family stores. We ate some food and walked the fairgrounds. Grandma Marie never bought anything at the craft booths. She always said it meant more to create those simple decorations yourself. It's what made a house into a home.

"Do you have a downtown like this in your hometown, Max?" asked Grandpa Frank.

"We used to, but there are more mini-malls now than mom and pop stores."

"That's the problem with the young people today. There is no sense of community. When I came to America, I had a family already here waiting with open arms to take care of me and my Marie. We had to stick together. Those Irish wanted us back on the boat."

"I remember reading about that. It must have been tough."

"A little." Grandpa Frank rubbed his chin. "No more difficult than young people today. At least Marie and I had people to take care of us, look out for us and show us the way. Today, you young people think you can do it all on your own. You live in a town with strangers, you have fancy storefronts, but you don't even know the people inside. Sometimes fancy isn't always better, capisce?"

"So, most of your friends no longer have the stores?"

"Yes, some have stayed in town. Some have gone to that place they call paradise."

"Heaven?" asked Max.

"No, Florida." Grandpa Frank gave a loud laugh. "I got you, yes?"

"Yeah, you got me."

"So, Elizabeth says you want to take my picture?"

"Yes." Max looked around for me.

"Yes," I answered, as I turned toward them. "Max is a great photographer and he is trying to capture the true essence of America."

"And I am this America?" Grandpa Frank stood tall and brushed the wrinkles from his shirt.

"I thought you could be one of the characteristics I was trying to capture. You know, the man who comes from Ellis Island and makes a new life for himself."

"What makes you think I started a new life?"

"Well, I just thought, you know you had to start all over again in a new country."

"I'm just teasing you, Max. I guess a young man like you would think that way. I look at my life and think I would have lived the same way in Italy."

"But Grandpa Frank," I interrupted, "I thought you said you came to America for a better life?"

"I came to America for better opportunities, yes. But I did not live any differently when I came to America. You see, you young people think how you live is what you have. I think how I live by what I do. When I come to America, I still love my wife and I raise my children and I am a good citizen. I would do that in Italy, too."

"I guess that counts as the speech for the day."

"No speech Elizabeth, just my true essence. You see Max, I learn quick, yes?"

"I guess you had to. How about that picture? I would like to take one of you sitting under your grapevine. I think it would be best to use the natural light, and the sun is perfect around this time of day."

"Sounds good to me. Let's walk home. I remember the first time someone took my picture. I was a young man and planning to leave Italy soon with my bride. My father wanted me to have a picture of us together in Italy before I sailed to America. He said he didn't want me to forget where I come from and the people who would always be praying for my protection and good life. We had a nice celebration that day and drank my father's wine. My father said I would never taste wine as good as the wine from his grapes in Italy. The photographer took a picture of us sharing that wine on that special day. It is the only picture I have of my father. I would often look at that picture when I was younger and wonder if my father was drinking his wine and talking to the men about his son who sailed to America. I wish he could have come to America and drank the wine made from my grapevine, but that never would be. He was happy in Italy and he died a happy man. I wish to die the same way, happy and with a glass of wine."

"Oh Frank, I think you can think of a better way to die than a glass of wine in your hands," scolded my Grandma Marie.

"I am an old man and I can choose how I wish to die."

"No, you're an old fool." Grandma Marie walked up the steps to their house.

"Come to the back, Max. I will show you my grapevine and you take the picture. That will give my Marie some time to miss me."

"This is a great spot for the photograph Elizabeth."

"I told you it was a great place. Too bad the trolley still didn't come by."

"What about the train?"

"No train either," answered Grandpa Frank.

"Let me get my equipment in the car and I'll be right back."

"Thanks for doing this, Grandpa Frank." I sat down next to him.

"No problem. I hope the book is good. Maybe your Grandma and I will see him on those television shows."

"That would be neat. You're a lot more positive than some of our family members."

"What's this? Are you feeling sad about something Elizabeth?"

"No, I just wish people would have a little appreciation for those who don't follow the common, everyday working world. You know, it takes a lot of time and just as much energy to write a book as my cousins probably spend at their jobs."

"Are you happy?"

"And sometimes people can be so critical and really have no knowledge and judge."

"Are you happy?"

"Of course I'm happy...I love what I do, I guess."

"No guess. Don't be so hard on yourself. People only criticize when they don't understand. If you are happy, they will see that and stop such nonsense."

"And if they don't?"

"Then they're not worth knowing, capisce? Why spend time on thoughts and worries about people who spend no thoughts and worries about you. I tell you what my father told me, yes? He said that when people are mean to you it is only because they do not know who they are and they are afraid of that, capisce? But you Elizabeth, you know exactly who you are. So spend time with people who know who they are, too. Look at Max, he knows he likes to take pictures. He seems comfortable with that. Maybe his father was hoping for a doctor and maybe his boss thinks he shouldn't take my picture, yes? But he is here, capisce. If you trust yourself, you will meet people who believe in you and you will achieve much....as much as you work for. Never forget to work hard, yes?"

"Always working hard."

"That is good. Hard work allows you to show pride instead of guilt when the job is done. I know of many people who stand alongside people when a job is accomplished, but they do not have the same look of pride on their face as the person who really got the job done."

"Been there." I recalled all the previous bosses who took credit for my work.

"No anger, Elizabeth. When you get angry, you waste time on people who don't care about you. Don't waste your time getting even, just get up. Get up and continue to do what you love. Everything else will happen. Everything happens for a reason. If you do what you love and keep your head up, you will meet new people and have opportunities come your way. But if you hold your head down and live a life you don't love, all those opportunities will pass you by. And that, Elizabeth, is a life wasted. And that would make my life a waste, too. You see, I came to America for you, for all my family. In America you have choices, so don't be afraid to make the choice that's right for you."

"And what if I make the wrong choice?"

"That's when you need to have faith," as your Grandma Marie always says. "Do you really think you are so great that you can mess up God's plan?"

"I guess when you put it that way."

"I put it that way. So, let's get some wine while Max gets his camera in place. We can go in the house and see if your Grandma Marie still loves me." He put his arm around me and we walked towards the house.

"Grandma, where are you?"

"I was just looking for that picture of your Grandpa with his father, right before we left Italy."

"I put it in the Bible," Grandpa Frank answered, as we walked into the parlor.

"Is it in good condition?" I sat on the couch and watched my grandparents take out the Bible from the cabinet.

"Here we go." Grandpa Frank cautiously picked up the photograph and brought it to me.

"Well, look at that. You were pretty cute back then."

"Yes, I was. Every woman in Italy wanted me. But of course, I only wanted you, Marie."

"Oh please, I don't believe I put up with you sometimes. Just think how old that picture is. And I can remember it like yesterday. Our families were so proud we were going to America. Nervous, too! I knew we would never see them again. What were we thinking, Frank."

"We were young; we didn't have to think. That's what's nice about being young; you have all the time in the world to try new adventures. You don't have enough wisdom to be scared."

"Someone scared about his picture?" asked Max, as he entered the parlor.

"No, we were talking about something else," I answered as I got up from the couch.

"Yes, the picture!" exclaimed Grandpa Frank. "Let me get a glass of wine first and I meet you outside, yes?"

Max and I both left the house to set-up the equipment.

"I think my Grandpa should sit near here, so you can get some of his flowers and the walking trail in the background."

"That's a great idea." Grandpa Frank approached us with three glasses of wine. "I work hard on those flowers for all the people to love as they walk by in the evening. I like to see their smiling faces."

"Well then, that settles it. You sit right here."

"Wait, Wait." Grandpa Frank gestured to each of us to take a glass of wine. "First we drink to this wonderful day and the good Lord blessing us with such wonderful grapes to make this beautiful wine."

"Here's to the good Lord." We all raised our glasses and took a sip of the wine. "May he bless my new book as well as he blessed Grandpa Frank's grapevine."

"Salute." said Grandpa Frank.

"Dad, whatever happened to that picture of Grandpa Frank with his Dad in Italy?"

"You mean the one with him holding the wine?"

"Yeah, I saw it once at their house. It was in their Bible."

"Oh I loved that picture, Vincent. It captured the simplicity of the time. I loved it so much and told Marie it would look great in my kitchen. She had a duplicate made. I'm waiting for my new wallpaper, so I can hang it up."

"Yes, dear," answered my father with a groan.

"Where is it now, mom?"

"It's in the pantry, I think."

I walked in the house and went straight to the pantry. There were a few boxes of knickknacks on the shelf. Then in the corner, I saw a picture frame. I couldn't believe my eyes. I lifted the 18x20 wooden frame and turned it over. There was the enlarged picture of a young Grandpa Frank with his father on a sunny afternoon in Italy.

"This is perfect," I thought out loud. "I'm actually looking forward to giving this eulogy now."

The Eulogy

I awoke that morning before my alarm went off. I always love when that happens. To start my day waking by my own means; having a few minutes to just listen to the morning songs of the birds. I feel like the day is filled with endless opportunities for me. I knew the day's events were already planned and it was a day of saying goodbye to one of the dearest people in my life. I stretched, got out of bed and walked over to my old desk. I pulled out the eulogy from under my laptop and rubbed my fingers over the page. I took a deep breath and asked God for strength. I slipped on a pair of jeans and a sweatshirt, grabbed a five-dollar bill on the dresser, put my hair in a ponytail, picked up the eulogy and quietly walked down the stairs. I put my sneakers on in the mudroom and walked out the back door. I strolled up Green Hill Drive and looked at all the homes in my old neighborhood. It's funny how even as an adult, you know time doesn't stand still, but you still see the old homes as they looked when you were a kid. As you walk by a certain corner, you remember it was the place you fell on your bike, or a neighbor's tree may have been third base during the neighborhood kickball games. My nostalgic walk has me wondering if the new owners will ever realize how many memories their house holds. I wonder if the neighborhood will once again be filled with children playing and neighbors creating friendships. I continued to walk downtown and bought a cup of coffee. The place was filled with mostly old men. I think the owner was surprised to see a young face so early in the morning. I paid for the coffee and sat at a table outside. Across from me, an elderly man reading the paper. The front page is always the same- a few people arrested, economy still sluggish

105

and politicians saying they have a solution if only the public will re-elect them. I started to wonder how many people would begin their morning by reading the paper if they knew it was their last day to live. I wondered what my Grandpa did on the last morning he was to have on earth. Was he happy? Was there something more he wanted to do? Was there someone he wanted to speak to one more time? I guess people who know they're dying have it lucky. They can get all their 'things' in order and fulfill their last wishes. I suppose if more people lived like they were dying, there would be a lot less anger in the workplace. Pharmaceutical companies would lose a lot of money on sleeping pills, because people would realize not to worry about the small stuff. Families would spend a lot more time being together; no planning big Disney trips, just being together would be sufficient.

I looked at my watch and realized everyone at the house would probably be in line for showers and eating breakfast. I finished my coffee and made a three-point shot in the garbage can. I picked up the eulogy and started to read it as I walked home. I could hear the sounds of cars driving by as I left downtown, but my eyes never stopped reading. My feet knew exactly where to go. I had walked home this way for so many years in my childhood, it just becomes instinct. I looked at the bold words in the eulogy: Letter from Momma... Flowers... Passion. I wondered what everyone at the church would think of my words about Grandpa Frank. Would they even remember what I said? As I approached Green Hill Drive, I stopped and took another deep breath. I looked up at the morning sky and saw the sun breaking through the clouds. I remember Grandpa Frank telling me that good people are like the sun and mean people are like storm clouds. Some people make a miserable day turn happy with their warmth and shine. Sometimes, the sun has to fight through dark and stormy clouds, but the sun knows if he keeps shining, those miserable clouds will go away. Then, other people who were afraid of the storm clouds will appear and smile at the sun. The sun must never give up, because if he does, the storm clouds will always hide the others who are not strong enough to shine like the sun.

"Welcome to L.A.," said the greeter from the Los Angeles Times to Max and me. It was the spring of 2002, and Max convinced me to take a sports assignment with him. I would be writing the article and he would be taking the pictures. I never cared for writing about sports, but it was two months for free in L.A. It was a paid writing assignment. I said yes.

"Good Morning," said Max. "So this is sunny L.A. Land of the movie stars."

"Yeah, you may see a few here. They're into this tennis stuff, especially if they need their face in the paper to promote an upcoming movie. My name is Jason and, if you need anything, just give a shout."

"Where can I plug in my laptop?"

"Over there, with the rest of the writers."

"Guess this means I'll see you later."

"Yeah, we'll meet up for lunch."

"A word to the wise," interrupted Jason as I started to leave. "Watch out for that one reporter in the blue shirt. She takes and never gives, if you know what I mean."

"Not a problem. Thanks for the heads up." I walked towards the reporter table.

"You can sit over here Elizabeth," said a voice from the other end of the table.

"Hey, talk about a small world." I rushed over to give a former co-worker a hug. "I can't believe it's actually you, Vicki."

"So how's New York? I've been dying for a good slice of pizza for two years."

"It's good. The past year has been a little crazy with everything that has happened. But the world keeps spinning."

"And it certainly spins here. If you want to live in make believe land, move to L.A. Some of the people here will even make a New Yorker look twice."

"Are you glad you took the job out here?"

"Yeah, my commute is long but I enjoy my assignments. I'm out of the office a lot and don't have to deal with those office politics. On these road assignments, you meet some of the same people every year and can catch up on things and make a few new contacts."

"Speaking of meeting new people, I was warned about the blonde in the blue shirt. What's up?"

"Oh yeah, she can be trouble. She'll talk to you and get all the info she can. Then, she will turn her back, write up a story and never give you any credit. Not much of a team player, but I guess nobody is anymore."

"I think there are one or two good people left."

"Are you suggesting we write a story together?"

"Why not? It will be fun. We'll get it done twice as fast and then we can have more time to check out Monterey."

"How about getting it done three times as fast?"

"And you are?" I asked with a smile, as I turned around and extended my hand.

"I'm Lindsey, and I just spent the last two days interviewing some of the player's families. We could write a great article about the personal side of the players and really give it a family theme."

"I think that sounds great." said Vicki. "Let's do it."

The three of us spent the rest of the day watching the competition and getting the final scores. We also compared notes during breaks and lunch. Max added some awesome pictures of the player's families, and we had a complete story to send our editors by late afternoon. As we were packing our equipment, I received a glare from the blonde woman I was warned about. She started to approach me. I gave Vicki a glance.

"You know," said the blonde woman as she placed her laptop on the table in front of me, "I couldn't help hearing your conversation and your approach to writing an article about this event. I just thought, as a veteran of journalism, I should let you know your editors will probably never accept such collaboration. I'm assuming you didn't get pre-approval and you are working with a novice." She glanced over at Lindsey.

"Better a novice than a bitch." I picked up my laptop and motioned to the girls to start moving.

"What would your Grandpa Frank say if I told him you swore?" laughed Vicki, as we all walked towards Max who was waiting by our rental car.

"He'd say sometimes you have to call them as you see them."

The four of us received an award the following winter for our collaboration on that article. We all met in Houston for the ceremony and had a blast celebrating at the hotel. We all send Christmas cards to each other. Lindsey is now a screenwriter in L.A. As my Grandpa Frank would say, just keep shining-because you never know what's waiting behind those storm clouds.

I entered the house and was greeted by my mother's panic. Nothing new. She was worried I had decided not to say the eulogy and maybe left for New York. Where mothers get these crazy notions, I haven't a clue. I decided to blame it on the high-cholesterol food we have been eating for the past few days.

"If you want a hot shower, grab it now." My Dad walked into the kitchen and threw his tie on the table.

"I'll make some breakfast while you get ready."

"I already ate downtown Mom. Don't worry about me. I'll be able to eat after the eulogy is done. Trust me."

I took a quick shower and put on a navy blue dress suit. I grabbed my favorite cross necklace to wear and carried it downstairs, along with my heels. I always wait to put on heels until the last minute. The less time I have to wear those things, the better.

"Dad, can you put on my necklace? My hands are too busy shaking."

"No problem. Stop being so nervous. Everything is going to be fine."

"Easy for you to say."

"It's easy for me to say, because I've seen you give speeches before. You get all nervous and then you get up there and you're fine."

"I want to make sure this speech comes out extra fine."

"Just remember, it's you and your Grandpa. When has he ever been disappointed by you?"

"Let's sit down and at least have some fruit."

"Really Mom, I'm good. I think I'll just sit outside for a little bit, until you and Dad are ready to go to the funeral home."

"I'll put a few plums in my purse in case you change your mind."

As I walked outside, I strolled towards the glider in the backyard. I sat down and concentrated on my breathing. I closed my eyes and pictured myself standing at the podium in front of all my relatives and my Grandpa Frank. I rehearsed my speech and visualized myself walking back to the pew and feeling good about a job well done. As I opened my eyes, I saw my father walking towards the garage. He looked good in his suit. I wondered what he has been thinking these past few days. I haven't seen him cry. I guess, as you get older, you accept the fact that every day with the people you love is a gift. You begin to understand how precious family moments are. You learn to distance yourself from the crazy things in the world that really don't matter. Looking back now, I think Grandpa Frank learned that lesson while he was still young. Lucky him. Lucky me for knowing such a wise man.

"Grandpa, were you always smart?" I asked with the inquisitive voice of a nine year old.

"I always thought I was." He laughed, while holding my skeleton mask to my Halloween costume. We walked up the steps to another spooky decorated house. "I guess everybody thinks they are smart, until they get old enough to know better."

"That doesn't make sense."

"Well, someday it will."

"Someday...someday....that is all my mom says when I ask her about stuff. Someday we will go to Disney Land...someday we will get a pool...someday."

"Sounds like you have a lot to look forward to."

"Funny." I gestured for my mask.

"Now don't forget to ask if your Grandpa can have a piece of candy too."

"Why don't you get dressed up?"

"Tricks are for kids," he laughed. "Get it? I love those silly commercials."

"You're becoming a real American."

"And I have the card to prove it. Oh yes, you little Elizabeth are very lucky to be born in such a country. In my country, nobody gave us free food."

"It's not food Grandpa; it's candy."

"Oh yes, yes. Here, put on your scary mask."

"Do you think I'm a baby for being too scared to wear the mask?"

"No, it is good for people to be scared of some things in life. It keeps them from getting too large headed."

"It's big-headed, Grandpa."

"Yes, you know this already. That is good. No more worrying about such little stuff. You will have much time to have big worries someday."

"There's that word again."

"Elizabeth." I turned around with my skeleton mask.

"Yeah?"

"Don't forget, I like Snickers."

I got in the car with my parents and Dad drove us to the funeral home. I asked him to stop at the drugstore. I had an idea for the eulogy and thought Grandpa Frank would have loved it. I ran into the store and quickly made my purchase. My parents looked at me kind of strange when I wouldn't tell them what was in the bag, but they have grown accustomed to my sometimes crazy behavior. They also knew I loved Grandpa Frank dearly, and would never do anything to embarrass him or the family on this memorable day. We arrived at the funeral parlor the same time as my Grandma Marie, who was driven by Uncle Dominick and Aunt Caterina. Aunt Caterina never drove much. She has her license, but it's with limitations. It all started back in 1979...

"What do you mean the weather is bad?" Aunt Caterina talked on the phone with her sister Marie.

"Frank thinks the roads are too bad and the storm is getting worse. They haven't even plowed our road yet. I don't think you will be able to drive to the house."

"We have to get our hair done today. We have a Rosary meeting tomorrow and Mrs. Ferrucci will be there and you know how she is."

"I know, but Frank thinks."

"I will be there as soon as I can. Just keep looking out your window for me." Aunt Caterina hung up the phone and quickly put on her winter coat and gloves.

"I don't believe she is driving in this weather. I don't want you in the car with that crazy woman."

"She's my sister, Frank. Do I talk about your brothers like that?"

"My brothers stayed in Italy. We should have never written to your sisters telling them how great it is in America. Maybe I would not have all this gray hair."

"Just stop getting all excited. You see, here she is now. I see her car and she is driving just fine. I need to get my coat."

"There is no need to get your coat." Grandpa Frank looked out the window. "That crazy woman just crashed into the telephone pole."

"Oh my God! Frank, go help her. Just don't stand here."

"What? I have to go outside and help a lady who doesn't know when you should stay home during a snowstorm? And just to get your hair beautiful? Is this why we come to America?" Grandpa Frank continued to complain as he put on his coat and walked towards the door.

"Frank, please."

"Yes, Yes. I am coming Caterina."

"Oh, I am so sorry Frank. I can't believe I hit the pole."

"Are you okay?"

"Yes, but we need to call the police right away."

"Of course. Yes, but first we will go inside and Marie is making some tea."

"Oh, that sounds good." They approached the house and Marie opened the door for them.

"Are you okay?" Marie asked her sister.

"I am fine. Just fine. I think the car is good, too."

"Yes, everything is fine," answered Grandpa Frank. "I think the car needs a tow truck to get out of that slope. I will call my friend Joseph while you sit with your tea."

"Oh yes, but I need to call the police first," Caterina answered as she walked towards the phone. "We will need a ride to the beauty parlor. Our appointment is for 11:00 and that tow truck will never get here in time."

"Caterina, the police are for emergencies."

"And this is no emergency, Frank?" Caterina dialed the telephone. "Yes, I need a ride by one of your policeman. I have an emergency and my car is stuck in the road. Yes. Yes. Oh, good. Yes, the address is..."

"I don't believe your sister." Frank sat at the kitchen table. "I can't wait to see the police man's face when he comes."

"Well, you know Caterina and her hair appointments."

"I know you." Caterina hung up the phone and joined them at the kitchen table.

After a few moments, Caterina saw the police car lights flashing from the window. The officer exited the car and walked towards the front door.

"Good Morning, folks," the young officer said. "What seems to be the emergency?"

"My sister and I have to get to an appointment by 11:00 and you are just in time."

"I see. Do you have a doctor's appointment ma'am?"

"No officer," interrupted Grandpa Frank as he gestured for the police officer to come inside out of the snow. "It is much more important than that. They have an appointment at the beauty parlor."

"Well, ladies, I'm really only supposed to transport people with emergencies."

"And this is an emergency," interrupted Caterina. "We have to get to the beauty parlor. Today is Wednesday and everyone will be there. We can't possibly miss our Wednesday and then expect to attend the Rosary Society the next day."

"And no gossip to share," murmured Grandpa Frank.

"Well, let me just call into the station. I'll be right back, unless of course you ladies have some type of limitations with your driver's license?" He smiled towards Grandpa Frank.

"Limitations, what does this mean, limitation?" asked Caterina.

"It means you can't do something," answered her sister, Marie.

"Well, yes young man, we have limitation. My car cannot go and we need to go. This is limitation."

"Yes, I suppose this one time you do have a limitation."

"Do you hear that Marie," interrupted Frank. "This one time you have limitation. After that, when it snows, your limitation is to just stay home, capisce?"

"Oh yes, well we can discuss that at the beauty parlor with the girls." Caterina put on her coat.

"Good luck young man," Grandpa Frank said to the officer, as he held open the door for Caterina and Marie.

"All in a day's work."

"Ah...I see you're not married."

"Huh?"

"Yes, you are not married."

"Good Morning Mom, did you sleep any last night?"

"A little. How is everyone doing at your place?"

"Good. Rose and her pack should be here soon," my mother answered.

"We wanted to get here early to check the flowers and make sure everything was just so," said my Aunt Caterina. She took Uncle Dominick's arm and started to lead everyone towards the entrance of the funeral home.

We entered the funeral home and proceeded to the room where Grandpa Frank was. In an odd way, it was comforting to know that I would still be able to see him today. As an adult, I know he isn't really with me, but just the presence of his body was eerily comforting. I took a seat behind the front row of chairs and bowed my head to say a silent prayer. I tried to concentrate on my breathing and hoped my body would begin to relax a bit before the eulogy. My thoughts took me back to the beach on Cape Cod the summer of my twenty-fifth birthday.

"Happy Birthday, Elizabeth." Grandpa Frank walked towards me on the beach at Cape Cod.

"I see you've come to join the early riser club." I took a sip of coffee and checked the view from my camera lens. "Unfortunately, we are the only members."

"I've always appreciated a good sunrise."

"I guess that's where I get it from then. Thanks."

"You know, Elizabeth, the beauty of the sunrise is a lot like death."

"What a nice morning conversation."

"You see, before the sunrise, everything is so dark and you are not sure what is out there. But then, you see these beautiful colors and your eyes say what a pretty light and the day is then filled with endless possibilities. I think that is what Heaven is, endless possibilities."

"That's a beautiful thought, Grandpa."

"Yes, once and awhile this immigrant is very impressive. I heard that word impressive from my friend Bob Steele many years ago on the radio. He was a good man. Taught me many English."

"I know, I remember your kitchen radio always being on when I was a kid."

"What do you mean, 'when I was a kid', you still are a kid."

"Well thanks, but according to many people, whom shall remain nameless, they think I'm getting old and should settle down, if you know what I mean." I took another sip of coffee.

"I don't like that phrase 'settling down'. When you marry, it should settle you up, capisce?"

"No, not really. No capisce."

"When you marry, it's about creating something better, building something with somebody. Your Grandma and me, we built a family together and that is something that you can never destroy. We never settle down, we are always building each other up, capisce?"

"Capisce. I guess I just don't think James is the right person I want to build up with for the rest of my life."

"So, what's the problem then?"

"What if he is the right person and I don't realize it until later?"

"Then you will find him again."

"And what if he's already married by then?"

"Then he wasn't the right one."

"You make it sound so easy."

"When something is right, you can feel it so passionately. It is like when you take the job in New York. Your parents were afraid at first, but because you felt so passionate about it, you just had to go and you knew you would make it work. It is the same with falling in love. If both people are truly passionate towards each other, that love will hold them together and they will become strong together. It's just faith in that feeling and each other."

"I guess that's my answer. People in this world can use a little more faith."

"Then why not start with you?" Grandpa Frank bent down to look through my camera lens.

116

"Yes, the man had a lot of faith." A stranger spoke to my Grandma Marie, as he shook her hand at the funeral parlor.

"Excuse me everyone," said the priest as he entered the room. "Could we all take a seat and bow our heads as we say a special prayer together before proceeding to the Church today."

"Elizabeth, how ya holding up?" asked my cousin Johnny, looking sharp in his Army uniform.

"I'm alright, just reminiscing a lot these past few days."

"Me, too. Are you ready to give the eulogy?"

"Yeah," I answered with a whisper, "but I sure could use some fresh air and some alone time."

"Consider it done." He leaned toward his mother and whispered something in her ear. "Follow me." He took my hand and we walked quietly towards the rear exit to the parking lot.

Once we got outside I took a deep breath and felt my body totally relax. I looked around at the crowded parking lot and the two police officers at the front of the car procession.

"Is that Elliot?" I gestured towards one of the police officers.

"Yeah. He came back to Southington a few years ago with a wife and three kids."

"Let's go see if he can do us a favor. He owes me one for always picking him first for kickball teams in the sixth grade."

"Well, if it isn't the Army hero and the New York writer."

"Hi Elliot," I said, while giving him a hug. "Sorry to meet you under these circumstances."

"Yeah, he was a great guy, always giving the kids candy. Sometimes I'd see him sitting under his grapevine when I had patrol duty in the old neighborhood. Now, I wish I got out of the car and said hello a few times."

"How about a favor?"

"Sure."

"A ride to the church? You'll be back in plenty of time before everybody leaves the funeral home."

"Well sure, I guess. But don't you want to say goodbye to your Grandpa Frank one more time?"

"I think it's more important that I took the time to say hello."

Johnny and I arrived at the church and thanked Elliot for the ride. We walked through the front doors of the church and heard the singers rehearsing in the balcony. One of my Grandpa's favorite songs was 'Take My Hand Precious Lord'. I knew there wouldn't be a dry eye in the house after the song was sung; which is why I requested the song be sung after the eulogy, not before. I sat in the second pew from the altar and Johnny joined me.

"It won't be much longer now," Johnny said.

"I remember when you said that a few years ago."

"Really? When?"

"I think it was 1978..."

"What are you going to tell him?" Johnny and I sat in the pew on a hot Saturday afternoon in the summer of 1978.

"I don't know, but I gotta give him something."

"Did you do any sins?"

"I don't think so, but the priest isn't going to believe that. Maybe we should both think of something to say and that way we won't tell him the same thing."

"Isn't it a sin to lie?"

"Yeah, but this way we'll be all set for next year because we can say we lied last year at confession."

"That's a great idea. I'll say I fought with my sister and didn't talk to her for a whole week."

"Cool. And I'll say I stole some money from my dad's wallet so I could buy a candy bar."

"Sounds good to me."

"And just in time, here comes the priest."

"Elizabeth...Elizabeth....here comes the priest," Johnny kept saying as he rubbed my arm.

"What? Oh sorry, I was just thinking about something."

"No doubt your Grandpa Frank's eulogy," answered the priest, as he sat in the pew in front of Johnny and me.

"Yes Father, how are you?"

"I am trying to prepare myself for the many people who will be filling these pews in a short time. Your Grandfather was a very well-loved man."

"You mean you still get nervous, Father?"

"Of course. Especially at funerals. I try to remember the grief the family is feeling and what words I can possibly say to them to provide some comfort."

"I'm sure you'll do just fine," answered Johnny.

"And you Elizabeth? What will you say to everyone to help capture your Grandpa Frank's spirit?"

"I guess you'll have to find out when everybody else does." We heard the cars entering the parking lot.

We joined the family beside the hearse carrying Grandpa Frank. The employees of the funeral home brought the flowers inside the church. Slowly, the pallbearers removed the casket and carried it towards the Church doors. They carefully wheeled the casket into the Church. Slowly, we all began to proceed behind the casket and walked inside the Church while the organ played. We all took our designated seats and waited for the priest to begin. This was it, the day that ends all days with my Grandpa Frank. From now on, I could only reflect on my memories. There would be no more new memories to make with my Grandpa Frank. I began to cry.

"And now, I will ask Elizabeth Manciano to say the Eulogy," I heard the priest say, as I returned from my thoughts.

I walked past the casket, up the steps towards the altar, and turned left towards the podium. Suddenly, I felt a deep sense of calmness over me. I took a deep breath and exhaled. I stepped in front of the podium and adjusted the microphone. I looked at my notes waiting there for me. I looked at everyone sitting in the congregation. I smiled, looked at my Grandmother and then began to speak.

"Hello everyone. I was asked to say a few words today about my Grandpa Frank. For those of you who know me, I'm sure you can imagine how thrilled I was to give a speech in front of so many people."

There was a polite chuckle and I relaxed some more.

"My Grandpa Frank is my hero. That probably sounds like the beginning of a speech that an eleven year old might say, but I guess, for me, I will always remember myself as a young kid when I recall my Grandpa Frank. In my opinion, I had the best childhood in the world, and it was mostly because of my Grandpa Frank. He taught me so many life lessons and not once were those lessons learned from lectures, shouts or in anger. Grandpa Frank taught me the important things in life through stories and his own actions...and that to me is a gift I hope to pass along someday. The love he had for his family surpassed any definition of unconditional love that I can think of to put in words for you today. His love came from the love he was given as a child and, I think, Grandpa Frank knew the importance of that love his parents gave him, and how necessary and valuable it was to share his love with his children and grandchildren. Recently, my Grandma Marie shared a letter with me. The letter was addressed to my Grandpa Frank and it was from his mother. The letter reminded my Grandpa of how much his parents loved him and to never forget how proud they were of him. The pride his parents expressed resulted in Grandpa Frank always living an honest and loving life in America. He came to America, he would say, with just the ownership of his last name, so he made sure it always maintained its value. I wonder how many of us would change our lifestyles and life choices if we had that kind of respect for our last names; for the respect of its' past owners, as well as the future recipients.

Grandpa Frank lived a passionate life. He cared about everything and everyone and was never too busy to make things just right or help people feel better. He loved his grapevine and surrounding it with the prettiest flowers. He taught me the secret of a good life through his flower garden and grapevine. You see, growing flowers is just like growing into your life. First, you have to prepare the ground for which you tend to grow in. You need a lot of different ingredients to make a rich soil, and sometimes the ingredients won't smell that good...but you need them all. Once you decide what you want to plant, you have to tend to it daily and provide nourishment and protection from any outside intrusions. At times, your flowers or grapes may seem stagnate, but keep at it, because one day you will turn around and find someone admiring what you have grown. You will share some joy and knowledge with that admirer and, maybe, a special love. A love that resulted from the passion you cultivated with time, respect and commitment.

The other day, my parents showed me a picture of Grandpa Frank. The photograph showed him standing by his father in Italy and pouring him a glass of wine. The picture was taken a few days before Grandpa Frank and Grandma Marie left for America. When I look at that picture, I see a young man with endless possibilities and a lot of faith. Since I know there is a priest nearby, I won't begin to preach about faith. But I can tell you about endless possibilities. A few years ago, I was at the Cape watching the sunrise one morning. Grandpa Frank walked over to me and he started telling me how he loved sunrises. He said watching the sunrise is good for the soul. It reminds us that the day is filled with endless possibilities and we can make anything happen if we work hard and have faith. In today's world, I think we get confused about working hard to be fulfilled and working hard to get ahead. As Grandpa Frank would say, if you are looking to get ahead, you must ask yourself who you want to get ahead of....but if you work hard to be fulfilled, you will find true happiness and faith.

I have so many stories, special memories, about my Grandpa Frank. I know every one of you could walk up to this podium and make us laugh, cry and maybe turn a shade of red with some of the adventures you shared with the man. I ask that you remember those times when you think of my Grandpa, not the memory of today. I thought today was a day of saying goodbye to him, but now I realize it's just another day of living a good life to represent a very proud and passionate man with a very valuable last name. A name I will continue to increase in value with my life choices and I hope you do the same.

I have compiled a top ten list of quotes I will always remember my Grandpa Frank saying to me. I am going to call this list the May you list, and once I began to read the list, you will understand why. I hope at least one or two may be helpful to you somewhere down the road. May you always remember your life choices become your lifestyle; May you always have someone to say 'I love you' to; May you have daily struggles that build soul not skepticism; May you have family that teaches you responsibility by letting you fall, and knowing when you really need to be picked up; May you surround yourself with friends who are constantly growing and willing to share their knowledge; May you always remember your life is never more important than anyone else's...anyone; May you always remember that life may be shaky at times, but your faith must never waver; May you always remember special moments aren't planned or postponed-so enjoy the interruption; May you always remember your actions become your family history; May you always remember anything you ever dreamed as a possibility may just become a reality with perseverance and passion.

One last thing before I go. My Grandpa Frank indeed taught me the important things in life. One of those things being the importance of candy...yes candy. Grandpa Frank never refused a child candy and I think, when it involves candy, we all remain children at heart. So, instead of passing the basket today for a collection, take a piece of candy and eat it right away...don't save it for a special day or worry about the calories. Just enjoy it like a child would...like my Grandpa Frank was sitting next to you with all the time in the world, under his grapevine."

Small Town Lessons

"Nice job today, Liz." My cousin Laura sipped her glass of wine.

"Thanks. I hope Grandma feels the same way. I haven't even gotten a chance to talk to her yet. Everyone has been crowding her since we got to the restaurant."

"I'm sure she liked it. When will you be returning to the big city?"

"Not sure. I have some article deadlines, but I can send them via e-mail from where ever. Thank goodness for laptops."

"So does that mean you will be staying in Southington for a while?"

"No. I was thinking of doing a little traveling this fall."

"I thought you've been everywhere," interrupted Nick, as he checked his cell phone for messages.

"Can't tear yourself apart from that thing?"

"Some of us have important clients to keep happy, my dear cousin."

"Right. Anyway, I was thinking of spending a little time out west and then maybe having Grandma come out to California. A friend of mine has a place out there in Monterey, and she said I could house sit for the month of October."

"Grandma Marie travel to Monterey? Are you crazy? She's too old for that type of stuff."

"Age is just a number, Laura. Besides, the weather may even make her feel better."

"Who needs to feel better?"

"Grandma Marie does Dad. I was thinking of inviting her out to Monterey in the fall."

"I bet she would like that. And, more importantly, it would give the ladies at the beauty parlor something to talk about."

"Then it's settled. I'll ask Grandma Marie tomorrow before I leave for Vermont."

"Vermont?"

"My friend Max is taking some photos of an old town and I'm writing some stories about the people there. One of those articles with the theme- 'remember what New England used to be like and how progress has eliminated so many small-towns and charming villages'. I got an e-mail from Max the other day. I thought, there will be so many people around Grandma the next week or so, she won't even know I'm gone."

"I guess you're right. She is a little crowded." He glanced over at the table where Grandma Marie was sitting, surrounded by her sisters and a few grandchildren.

"I'll tell her a little later about my plans. Right now, I'm going for seconds at the buffet table."

"Me too." Johnny grabbed his plate and led the way.

"So what are your plans?" I asked Johnny, as we loaded our plates with Italian food.

"Back to the Army life at Fort Bragg for another year, and then who knows."

"Have you given any thought to what you'll be doing in the civilian world?"

"I like being outside and I always enjoyed working with my hands. So, maybe something in construction or landscaping."

"You should plan a trip to California and check the opportunities out there. Nobody does their own landscaping in those posh neighborhoods."

"Maybe I'll do that."

"Do what?" interrupted Aunt Betty, Johnny's mom.

"Check out the job market in California."

"Oh my, I was hoping you would come back to Southington when your time with the Army was over."

"Mom, what can I do here? Besides, it's pretty difficult living on military paychecks in Connecticut."

"And California is cheaper?"

"I just said I was going to check it out. Actually, I was thinking of Montana."

"Why Montana?" I interrupted.

"A buddy of mine just bought 200 acres out there and he's going to raise buffalo. You should see the pictures he sends me of his place. He's built a nice home for his family, and there's a little cabin he's offered to me until I find something permanent."

"Sounds like a great offer."

"Not to me," answered Aunt Betty. "We don't have any family in Montana. And to be in the wilderness like that."

"It's not like there are still cowboys fighting Indians, mother. Besides, I know one person out there, and I hear there are many more people there who speak English."

"Very cute. I don't know where you kids get these foolish ideas. Eventually, you have to accept that life isn't one big thrilling adventure all the time."

"I know someone who would disagree," I answered. "That is, someone I once knew."

It was the spring of my college graduation and I was ready to take some time off before entering the 'working world'. I had been in the military world for two years, the academic scene for three years, and now, I just wanted to be on my own for a while. My parents thought I was nuts when I put everything in storage, packed my car with the basic necessities and planned a cross-country trip for the next three months. For the first time in my life, I had no one to report to, worry about or deadlines to meet. I was thrilled to be driving in my car, just exploring every city and small town across America. I had my camera and my laptop to capture every moment. I was living the American dream. At least, I thought so. My folks had a different opinion, but fortunately Grandpa Frank was there for support and guidance.

"Do you have plenty of film?"

"Yes Grandpa Frank, I have enough film to get me through the first month."

"Good. Make sure you take plenty of pictures. I always wanted to see the cowboys out west. You take a picture of a cowboy for me, capisce?"

"Capisce." I put the last suitcase in my car.

"Here's a little something for the road." My mother held the back door open for my dad, as he placed a box of food in the back seat.

"Mom, there will be restaurants along the way, you know."

"And hotels with phones," added my father. "Make sure you call every night. Collect if you have to- got it?"

"I got it; I got it. Don't worry, I will be fine."

"That's right. My little Elizabeth knows how to take care of herself," interrupted my Grandpa Frank. "And what she doesn't know, she will learn on this trip, yes?"

"It is the best way to learn about this country."

"Exactly Vincent. But that doesn't mean your momma won't stop worrying. You call every night and we all sleep well."

"You have the map?"

"Right by the driver's seat, Dad."

"Have a safe trip and remember we love you. That is why we worry so much." My mother gave me a hug.

"Tell the Grand Canyon I said hello." My dad hugged me next.

"Your Grandma Marie and I wanted to give you a little spending money." He put an envelope in my coat pocket and kissed me goodbye. "Maybe, if you remember, you bring back some of that California sand?"

"I'll remember." I got into my car and started the engine.

I waved goodbye and drove down the driveway. Within minutes, I was on Highway 84 West on my way to Interstate 80. My goal for the first day was to travel across Pennsylvania and make a few stops for some pictures here and there. I felt quite proud when four o'clock arrived and I was almost at the border. I decided to take a detour through a small town and try to find a place to stay for the night. The end of the exit brought me to a quaint village with a downtown that reminded me of the 1960's era. There was a pharmacy, small grocery store, two screen movie theater, one gas station that was full-serve and a cozy little restaurant with some outside seating. There was a sign stating a Comfort Inn was two miles down the road, so I decided to check it out. Upon arrival, I decided it was clean and safe, so I registered, unpacked my car and made a quick phone call to my folks. Afterwards, I grabbed my coat, camera and purse and decided to walk back downtown. After nine hours in the car, walking sounded like a wonderful idea. I arrived in the downtown area quickly and grabbed some literature and maps at one of the antique stores. Most of the stores were just about to close, so I decided to grab a table on the patio at the restaurant and have a nice dinner.

"Have you decided what you'd like for dinner tonight," the middle-aged waitress said to me.

"Yes, the house special looks great and I'll have an iced tea to drink." I looked up from the literature I had taken from the antique shop.

"I guess it's that time of year again. People enjoying iced tea with the arrival of spring. And summer will be here before you know it."

"Well, I hope it doesn't go by too fast. I've been looking forward to this summer for the past five years."

"What do you mean?"

"I spent the first two years after my high school graduation in the service. I spent the next three years in college. But, all along, I knew I would get a chance to travel someday. Here I am on the road for the next three months."

"Why, lucky you. I've always dreamed of just packing my things and hitting the open road myself. But, life just seemed to get in the way."

"Well, this is my life for the next three months and your town is my first stop."

"What made you stop here?"

"It just seemed like a cute town from the highway. In the morning, I hope to get some great pictures of the sunrise over the fields."

"Well, I wish you luck on your trip. I hope you enjoy our little town and the cooking."

I smiled at her and looked back at the literature I was reading. One of the pamphlets mentioned an antique store a few miles down the road that I could stop at tomorrow morning. I decided to grab a pen in my coat pocket and place an asterisk next to the store name. As I reached in, I felt the envelope my Grandpa Frank gave me that morning. I pulled it out and opened the envelope. There was a letter wrapped around some money. I carefully placed the money back in my coat pocket and read the letter.

Dear Elizabeth,

Your Grandma and I are so proud of you. We have been blessed to watch you go from a little girl to a beautiful young lady. We will pray for you while you are on your trip and far away from family. Have a good time and take many pictures for us. Make sure you use the money in this letter to buy a glass of wine at least once a day. The glass of wine will remind you to slow down, enjoy where you are and appreciate how far you have come. When you come home, your Grandma and I will have a glass of wine waiting for you under the grapevine.

God Bless-Grandpa Frank & Grandma Marie

"Here you go miss, one iced tea."

"Can I change that to a glass of blush wine?"

"Of course you can. A glass of wine sounds like a good idea on such a beautiful spring evening."

I smiled in agreement.

"Elizabeth, so what do you think? Elizabeth?"

"About what?" I looked around to remind myself where I was.

"Montana? What do you think of the deal with Montana? Should I go?"

"I think you should go back to Fort Bragg, finish your time and then spend your first day of civilian life on the road west."

"On the road west to California?"

"On the road west to a restaurant in some small town where you could just put your feet up, have a nice meal at a restaurant and enjoy a glass of wine."

"And then what?"

"And then you'll know what to do."

"How can you be so sure?"

"Because the best things in life happen when we are patient, prepared and passionate about something. Grandpa Frank would say the ingredients for a good life are the same as needed to make good wine." I excused myself and walked towards Grandma Marie at her table.

"May I join you?"

"Why, there you are."

"You're a hard lady to get alone."

"Oh, everybody has been so kind and they all have been saying what a nice job you did. I'm sure your Grandpa Frank was smiling, because of all the nice things you said about him."

"Well, I'm kinda glad it's over. You know public speaking isn't my favorite thing."

"So, what's next on your writing ticket?"

"I'm glad you asked. My friend Max and I are working on a project together in Vermont. He's actually picking me up tomorrow morning. After that, I have a pit stop to make in New York. Then, it's off to Monterey to complete my next book."

"Oh, I didn't know you were writing another book?"

"Well, if you promise not to tell anyone, I actually only have an idea for a book. The hard part is sitting down and getting it on paper. I think Monterey will be the perfect spot for some quiet and relaxation."

"Sounds like you've got it all planned."

"There's just one more thing. I was wondering if you'd like to come visit me in Monterey? It will be great! I'll be house sitting for a friend the entire month of October. You can come any time and stay as long as you want."

"Are you sure you wouldn't mind me tagging along?"

"It will be great. You always said you wanted to see the Pacific Ocean. This is your chance."

"Well, I suppose I can get my hair done the beginning of the month and stay with you for a week or two."

"I'll get you a ticket for two weeks, and if you decide to leave early we'll just change it. No big deal. I'll have you fly in to San Jose and I'll be waiting for you. You'll love the drive to Monterey."

"I can't believe I'm actually doing this," Grandma Marie said with a mix of excitement and guilt.

"If you need to talk to me while I'm in Vermont, just call my cell phone. If you have a problem, just call my Dad. He knows how to get in touch with me at all times through my editor."

"California here I come!"

The next morning, I awoke at six o'clock and took a shower. I put on my favorite pair of jeans and a sweatshirt. The fall season was just beginning, and I loved this time of year in New England. You can wear a sweatshirt, but still no bulky coat or hat & gloves. I was anxious to drive to Vermont and interview some people. If I had my choice, I'd spend all my time traveling and just meeting new people every day. I think it's the best way to learn. I quietly walked downstairs with my suitcases, and then got a startling surprise. My Mom and Dad were sitting at the kitchen table with a steaming plate of pancakes and bacon.

"You didn't think we'd let you leave without a good breakfast?"

"Thanks Dad. I just figured I'd get something on the road."

"Nonsense. Besides, when has Max ever been on time?"

"You got a point there, Mom."

"So, tell us about this trip to Vermont," said my Dad.

"There's not much to tell. Max will be taking the photographs and I will be interviewing members of the community. We have about six or seven small towns to visit on our list, so they know we are coming. The main theme of the article will be how these quaint New England small towns are disappearing and maybe finding ways to preserve their existence."

"It sounds like a good idea," interrupted my mother. "Everything seems to be changing so fast in the name of progress. It's nice to keep some things the same."

"Well, I'll see what I can do."

"Do about what?" Max let himself in the back door.

"Oh my God, you scared me," I answered with a shriek.

"I saw the kitchen light on and your father sitting at the table. I guess Elizabeth got everyone up this morning. Pancakes!" Max sat at the table and grabbed a plate.

"Don't be so shy, Max."

"You go right ahead and eat as much as you want. You don't know what kind of food you'll get on the road."

"I'm sure the restaurants in Vermont have all been cleared with the health department, mother."

"All right, just finish your breakfast. It's probably best if you leave here after eight o'clock. The traffic in Hartford from six to eight o'clock is ridiculous."

"Good plan, Mr. Manciano. That gives me time to have seconds."

"So, your grandmother mentioned about going to Monterey."

"She and Grandpa always wanted to see the Pacific Ocean. I think she'll have a great time. It will be good for her to get away for a while."

"I think it's a lovely idea. Your father and I loved it there. I'll give your grandmother the name of a restaurant we ate at; the food was spectacular. We should also get her some new suitcases, dear. Lord knows she probably has the same suitcases they took from Italy to Ellis Island."

"And Grandpa Frank would probably say, 'why are we getting new suitcases...these still do a good job."

"None the less, we will take her shopping. Your father is going over there later to make sure she isn't alone. You should probably make a schedule for her on her calendar, so she knows who is visiting her on what days."

"Yes, dear."

"Well, it looks like we are ready. Right, Max?"

"Yeah, I guess we should be going. I would like to get to the first town by early afternoon and settle in the hotel. That will give us a chance to check out the town and plan what photos I need to take."

"Sounds good to me." I reached for my suitcases. "Tell Grandma I'm looking forward to California."

"I will," answered my dad, as he kissed me goodbye.

"Drive safely and be careful," advised my mother, as she kissed me goodbye.

"We will," I answered, as I closed the trunk of Max's car. "I'll be back in two weeks. Feel free to drive my car, just make sure I have a full tank when I return."

The drive to Vermont was beautiful. Always is this time of year. While Max drove, I stared out the window and got lost in my own thoughts. As we passed the trees with all their changing colors along Route 7, I started to think about my Grandpa Frank. He loved this time of year and I loved helping him rake the leaves and preparing the yard for the long winter season.

"Grandpa Frank, are we having Thanksgiving at your house?" I asked, as we piled the leaves into the vegetable garden.

"I don't think so, Elizabeth. I think your momma will be cooking the turkey this year."

"How come we can't have it at your house? I like having it here," I responded with a somewhat whiney fourteen year-old voice.

"Well, I think your Grandma Marie and I have decided to 'pass the torch' as they say here, right? And, your mother is a great cook. I'm sure we will have a wonderful Thanksgiving Day."

"I guess, but I still wish we were having it at your house."

"Life is about trying new things. That is how we learn, capisce?"

"What if I don't want to learn anymore new things?"

"Then you are dead."

"Oh, that's a nice comment Grandpa."

"It is true, no? If you are not learning and thinking, you are going nowhere."

"You and Grandma don't learn anything anymore. You already know everything."

"You say that because you think we are old, and maybe you are right. Yes, your Grandma is old. But, we still learn new things every day. Sometimes, as you get older, you see the things that have been around you all your life in a different way, too. Look at all these leaves, Elizabeth. When I was a young man, I looked at these leaves and thought 'I have to spend my Saturday raking all these leaves.' Now, I look at these leaves and think, I got to spend a beautiful summer and fall with my family. I hope the Lord lets me see the leaves blossom again in the spring."

"That's creepy."

"That's life. Always be looking and learning. You can always learn something where ever you are. Now, let me show you how we use these leaves to protect Grandma Marie's beautiful roses, yes?"

"Alright. And then maybe we can convince Grandma to come to my house and teach my mother how to make the stuffing the right way?"

"Hmmm...that we can do, but very carefully. Oh yes, with that situation, you will learn from your Grandpa Frank how to be a smooch talker."

"I think you mean smooth talker." We walked towards the rose bushes with our rakes in hand.

"Oh yes, smooth talker. You see, you already know. Yes, this is good."

"Hey, are you with me?" asked Max, as we approached the Vermont border.

"Huh," I said as my mind drifted back to the real world.

"I thought we drove together so we could strategize a bit, right?"

"Yeah, sorry. What time is it?"

"It's time for lunch. As soon as I see a town, we are pulling over."

"Sounds good to me. I think I could use another cup of coffee."

"Did you get any sleep last night?"

"Some, but things have been a little different these past few days."

"Yeah, I'm really sorry you lost your Grandpa, Elizabeth. I know you really liked him. Are you sure taking this assignment was the right thing?"

"Yes. There is really nothing for me to do back in Southington. Everyone will be visiting my Grandma. I think, by the time I return, she will need a break from my Aunts."

"I think you make a good point." Max pulled into a restaurant parking lot.

Max and I stayed at that restaurant for a good hour and had a nice, leisurely lunch. We talked about the article and what types of questions to ask the residents. I always liked traveling up North and meeting the real 'Yankees' of New England. Some towns have residents whose ancestry goes back eight or nine generations to the same town. It amazes me how some people just never opt to leave their hometown. However, once I started talking to a few 'old-timers', I realized they like things just the way they are, and plan on keeping it that way. Our first town had a population of 235 residents. We decided to drive to the next town, because it was the only one with a hotel in a forty-mile radius. We got our rooms and unpacked our things. We would be staying for the next few days. After about thirty minutes of getting some away time from Max, I decided to call his room and ask if he wanted to check out the town with me. He agreed, and within twenty-minutes, we met up in the lobby. We walked about the town and checked out some antique shops. The owner of one antique shop is the lady I will be interviewing the day after tomorrow. I figured if I introduced myself to one person in the town, that would take care of all the rest of the people I would be meeting to interview. In a small town, I think it's safe to say, everybody knows 'what's new' within a thirty-minute time frame. I was quite confident, once I left Kathy's antique shop, she would give all the necessary details about me to her friends. Then, the phone chain would continue.

After Max was comfortable with a list of locations he had planned to photograph in the morning, we walked back to the hotel. It was about four o'clock, so we decided to enjoy the pool for about an hour and then get ready for dinner. There were two restaurants in town and one at the hotel; all closing at eight o'clock. We decided to stay at the hotel restaurant and enjoy some wine and food until closing time. After that, Max decided it was best for him to return to his room and settle in for the night. He would be up early to take some photographs of the sunrise. We planned to meet for breakfast at nine o'clock tomorrow morning.

I took a stroll around the hotel by myself and checked the place out. I always love staying in hotels and watching the people come and go. I think about what their life may be like, why they are traveling and the stories they must have from their travels. If the writing career in New York ever becomes stagnate, I often thought of owning a little hotel or inn by the water. That way, the stories, or the people, would come to me and I could just write by the sea. Maybe someday, I thought, it would be a reality. For now, my job was to write about small towns in Vermont. My stroll had me arrive at the guest office room, where there were some computers. I decided to check my e-mail and maybe surf the web a bit. The first few e-mails were from my nervous editor in New York, which I quickly responded with a 'Don't Worry...Got It....or a Thanks for Sharing, I'll Keep that in Mind.' I scanned down the rest of the e-mails and noticed one from my cousin, Johnny. I was instantly intrigued, since Johnny hardly ever e-mails me, and quickly opened the letter. It read:

Hi Elizabeth! I'm sure you are surprised to get an e-mail from me ☺ I just wanted to say thanks for the advice the other day. I've decided to go for it, and travel west to Montana after my time in the Army is completed. You were right, I've got nothing to lose and if I don't try it, I'll always regret it. I guess we've come a long way from our small town in Connecticut. Some of our cousins may not think so- living the so-called suburb life with their McMansions and fancy cars! I guess, there comes a time when we have to ask ourselves what makes us happy and not worry about what the other guy thinks. Well, I hope Vermont is fun (as fun as Vermont can be) and I'll keep in touch. Your Cousin, Johnny

I closed the e-mail and smiled. 'Good for him', I said to myself. It's funny how we always say that about people who follow their dreams. We admire the people who take chances, and then return to our own unhappy place of work. The excuses we give range from 'gotta make the mortgage payments' to 'I've got kids to support.' I often wonder how many people are really stuck in their jobs and how many are really just scared to take responsibility for their own destiny. I started to surf the web and typed in Monterey. I made reservations at one of my favorite restaurants and requested a table with a view of the ocean. I wanted my Grandma Marie to have the best experience while on vacation. I also made reservations at a quaint tearoom in Carmel. I was starting to get excited about this trip and anxious to complete my writing assignment here in Vermont. I started to remember an Easter morning when my Grandpa Frank reminded me of the importance of not wishing time to move faster.

"How does it feel not to wear Army boots today?" asked Grandpa Frank, as he walked into the kitchen.

"Great. I almost forgot what sneakers felt like." I ate an Easter egg and sipped my coffee.

"So, how are you doing Elizabeth?"

"I'm okay. I enjoy my job and I've met some great people. I've also lost a few friends, but I guess that's to be expected with the situation we're in today."

"Yes, I suppose in some ways you have grown up faster than most nineteen year olds. Maybe, that's a good thing."

"How can losing a friend be a good thing?"

"You realize how precious time is. You understand how to enjoy the moment, because you realize how special that one moment is, capisce?"

"I guess. But it still doesn't seem fair."

"Ah, as you get older, you will also not get so angry about what is not fair. You see, sometimes what we think is not fair or too hard is really something important that God is teaching us or preparing us for. When you do not become so angry about everything that is not fair and just keep doing the best you can, you will understand why that moment was so special someday."

"Someday. I used to hate that word when I was a kid."

"Because you were a kid. Now, you have seen much and you have learned much. You have an edge, isn't that what they say-'edge'? You have an edge on most of the other kids your age. Make sure you use that when you have decisions to make. Most importantly, make sure you live everyday thinking about how lucky you are to have the gift of time."

"Well, after three months, I'll have all the time in the world. I'm still not sure how I'll use it. I think I need to make a plan. Make sure I have some security, you know."

"Your security is your faith and only you can give that away. If you need a plan, then go ahead and make a plan. Just remember, it may not match someone else's plan."

"Well, I gotta have some type of outline, Grandpa Frank. You just can't live every day without a care in the world."

"I didn't say not to care. I just said to enjoy the day. Some people live everyday according their plan, and they live it without a care for anyone or anything. Is that what your plan is?"

"Well no. I just meant."

"I know Elizabeth. Your Grandpa Frank is just trying to make you use that brain of yours, capisce? Always remember, your Grandma Marie and I came to America because we wanted to live a good life. We had some hard times, but we got through, and so will you. Just be patient and be thankful for every moment."

"I sure would be thankful for another cup of coffee."

"That, I can do."

Before I knew it, my alarm clock was sounding. It was time for our first day of work in Vermont. I stumbled to the shower and slowly came to life. I got dressed and put on my warm leather coat. The fall mornings in Vermont can be chilly, and since the sun hasn't even woke up yet, I knew a warm coat was a good idea. My phone rang once, which was Max letting me know he was leaving in five minutes. I had slid a note under his door last night asking him to ring my room once in the morning, and if I wasn't outside in five minutes, he could drive away. I grabbed a small bag with some snacks and my writing pad. I met Max in the parking lot and we said our half-awake good mornings and got in the car. Max drove down a one-lane dirt road to an old apple farm. It looked a bit spooky in the darkness, but one could see the sun beginning to peek over the mountains.

"Looks like it's going to be a great day." Max unpacked his equipment.

"Yeah, I love the sunrises. I'm glad I decided to come along."

"Me too. You'd be surprised how many looks I get from people when I'm up this early in the morning. Sometimes I wonder if they think I'm a criminal or something."

"Well, you know how it is in these small, Yankee towns. If they don't know you, they don't want to talk to you. No outsider, rich yuppy coming in and creating some progress."

"You think you'll have a hard time getting some interviews?"

"No, the magazine has done most of the scheduling. And, I think no one will mind complaining about how 'outsiders' keep coming in and buying their land to build summer mansions or strip malls."

"You got a point there." Max checked the view from his camera. "Looks good, now all I have to do is wait for the sun."

"Wow, your job is easy."

"Very cute."

"Just kidding. I think I'll do a little exploring down the road. Now that the sun is coming out, things don't look so spooky."

"Watch out for the boogie-man."

I walked down the dirt road towards a house past the apple farm. It wasn't your typical New England farmhouse that you see in the movies, just a modest house with chipped white paint and some shutters in need of repair. As I got closer to the

138

house, I noticed a light was on in one of the upstairs bedrooms. A figure walked by the window and I stopped. A moment later, the figure appeared again, carrying a baby. The figure pulled back the curtain and looked towards me. It was a mother holding her child, obviously just waking up to start the day. I gave a wave and she waved back. I pointed over the hill behind me to Max. You could see his silhouette now. She gave a smile, as if to say she remembered Max from yesterday when he asked if he could photograph their fields. She gestured to wait a moment and then disappeared from the window.

"Hello," said the lady as she opened the front door. She held her baby close to her chest and asked me to sit down with her on the front porch. "My husband is making some coffee. He'll be out in a few minutes."

"That sounds great. Max will be jealous."

"Max? Oh, is that the photographer?"

"Yes."

"Well, when he's done with his pictures, he is more than welcome to a cup. Are you two together?"

"Yeah, we work a lot of assignments together. He's easy to get along with."

"Oh, so you're not married?"

"Heck no, that's funny. No, Max and I are strictly business. Maybe that's why we get along so well."

"Maybe. So, I guess you do a lot of traveling?"

"Yeah, I love being someplace new every day and meeting new people like yourself. If you tell me your name, I can look on my list to see if I'll be interviewing you. My name is Elizabeth."

"The name is Nicole and I can guarantee I'm not on your list. I saw the advertisement a while back in the Village Newspaper looking for interested candidates. I thought to myself, 'why would a reporter want to interview me. All I know is this village. Haven't really traveled any farther than Rutland to be honest. And, to top it all off, I married my high school sweetheart."

"I think you're pretty typical Americana."

"Really, I would never guess that from watching television."

"Don't believe everything on t.v. Besides, everybody thinks the country is centered on New York and L.A. To be honest, I think most of this country is made-up of folks just like you. Don't sell yourself short."

"Well, it would be nice to see New York someday. Aren't you from Manhattan?'

"Yeah, it's where I live now, but I grew up in Connecticut."

"Coffee anyone?" spoke a young man, as he opened the porch door.

"Elizabeth, this is my husband Matthew."

"Nice to meet you Matthew. Thanks for the coffee."

"We need to save some for her friend Max. He's the one over there taking pictures of the sunrise."

"Not a problem," answered Matthew. "You know, I see that sunrise every day, and never really thought about taking a picture of it."

"I guess when you see something every day you tend to take it for granted. Plus, you know us artistic nerds."

"We get a few artists here in the summer time with their canvases. They tend to keep to themselves. I guess they enjoy the peacefulness that you don't find in the city."

"I bet you're right. Do you two enjoy the peacefulness? Or did that end with the new baby?"

"I guess a little of both," answered Nicole. "I love the idea of raising our children on a farm. But sometimes, we see our old high school friends return home for the holidays and they tell stories of their exciting careers and glamorous trips."

"Yeah, sometimes it would be nice to get in the car and go," added Matthew. "But, we have a farm, and a baby, too."

"And she's a cutie!" I added. "I hope I guessed right. I'm looking at the pink blanket."

"She's a girl," Nicole quickly responded. "And I know what you mean, that awkward moment when you're not sure. That's why I try to dress her with some 'girl colors.' Although, Matthew would love to put her in a flannel shirt."

"The next one will be a boy."

"You plan on having a lot of kids?"

"We would like four. I think that's a nice number. They will always have someone to play with."

"And to help their old man on the farm."

"If they want, dear."

"Sounds like you've got a plan."

"God willing," said Matthew.

"You sound like my Grandpa Frank. He always believed there was someone greater than us with the ultimate plan."

"Sounds like a good guy. Does he live in New York?"

"No, he actually died a week ago in Connecticut. Max picked me up at my folks' house the day after the funeral."

"Oh, I'm sorry to hear that, Elizabeth. It must be hard going back to work."

"A little. But I'm taking my grandmother on a trip to California after I complete my job here. So, we are both looking forward to that."

"California. Someday Matthew, I want to go there and see the Pacific Ocean."

"Someday." Matthew sipped his coffee and peered over my shoulder.

"You've got a nice looking farm here," said Max, as he approached the front porch.

"Thank you." Matthew handed Max a cup of coffee.

"I think I got one or two good pictures. I'll see how they look on the computer when we get back to the hotel."

"You are your own worst critic, Max. I'm sure they all look great."

"Well, thanks Elizabeth. Have you been pestering these folks for an interview?"

"Not yet. Max, this nice couple is Nicole and Matthew. And their baby girl- what's her name?"

"Olivia."

"Olivia. What a pretty name. I hear it quite often now. I guess it's making a comeback."

"Everything goes in a circle," answered Matthew. "Just like this town. People worry that it may wither away to a ghost town if big business isn't allowed in. That has been the same concern my grandfather and his grandfather have shared. Somehow, we always seem to get by and make do with what we have. I think it's just about knowing what you want and having what you need."

"Very well said." Max lifted his coffee cup in the air, as if to give a toast.

"Well, the sun is awake and that means the hotel restaurant should be awake, too. I think we better pack-up your equipment and head back to town."

"Sounds like a plan, Elizabeth. It was nice meeting you folks."

"Same here," said Matthew, as his wife Nicole smiled. "Maybe we'll see you at the town fair a week from Saturday?"

"I didn't see any advertising for a fair."

"There is no advertising," laughed Nicole. "It's just the townspeople getting together at the park by the pond. Everyone brings something to eat. We just sit, talk and catch-up on things."

"It's nothing fancy, but the food is great," added Matthew.

"Well, we have to come back this way on the trip home, so maybe you'll see us. I guess it depends on how much we get done in two weeks, or if we need the weekend to finish the story."

"Always that deadline." Max shook Matthew's hand and waved goodbye to Nicole.

"Good luck on your stories," said Nicole.

"Thanks. And have fun taking care of that cute baby girl."

The rest of the day I spent interviewing townspeople and asking them what they liked most about their small town. Around noon, I had a good ninety minutes before my next interview, so I decided to have lunch at the local restaurant. Although most people hate to eat alone, I quite enjoy it. When you're alone, you have the opportunity to watch the people and wonder about the life they live. It's always a plus when you meet a friendly waitress, too. I believe if you want to know anything in a hurry about a town, just ask a waitress or a hairdresser.

I sat at a table by the front window with my Village Newspaper. Just as I opened it, a waitress approached with a smile.

"Nothing much exciting in there, sweetie. You should have brought your New York Times with you," she said jokingly.

"How did you know I was from New York?"

"You interviewed my mother's sister this morning."

"Oh, is she here now?"

"No, but her husband's brother is, and they're neighbors. But actually, Patty told me. Patty owns the diner and she is the daughter of the brother who lives next door to my mother's sister."

"Got it...I think."

"Can I get you something to drink?"

"How about a Coke and a cheeseburger."

"Sure. Fries or chips?"

"I'll take the fries."

"Alright, just give me a few minutes and I'll bring that right out."

I sat and read the Village Newspaper as I waited for my meal. The waitress was right, not much happening in town. There were a few articles about school news and some property transfers. I started to read an article about fishing, but then an older couple at a corner booth caught my eye. I must have been staring for a while, because the waitress approached and gave her two cents about what she guessed I was thinking.

"Don't even think about it." She placed my cheeseburger and fries in front of me.

"What do you mean?"

"I mean about interviewing that old couple over there. They are the Millers, and Mr. Miller could care less about having his name in some fancy New York paper."

"What's the matter with him?"

"Well, I'm not one to gossip." She sat down in the chair across from me. "It's been rumored that Mr. Miller hasn't left any of his land to his kids...and honey, that's a lot of land."

"Why not?"

"Because he doesn't trust them. He thinks they'll sell it and buy some fancy home in the suburbs. Mr. Miller's land goes back generations. It would break his heart if it left the family."

"So, whom did he leave the land to?"

"From what I hear, after he and his wife die, the land is given to the village to be used as a park, with all those fancy nature trails that you city people like to come to once a year and get one with nature."

"I guess that sounds like a good idea."

"No, it's not. You see the Miller land is like half the town. So, if that land can never be sold, than there is no way this town will ever grow and prosper."

"What's your definition of prospering? Some people think the town is fine the way it is."

"Well, some things about this place are good. But for me, it would be nice to meet some new people now and then. Like you, I bet you've got a bunch of stories in your head from all the people you have met."

"That's true, but I've traveled a lot, too. What's stopping you from getting out on life's big highway?"

"Two kids, back child support and being the only waitress at the only diner in town."

"That would do it."

"How's the cheeseburger?"

"So far, the two bites I've had our delicious."

"You're funny. I bet you do well on those interviews."

"I always try my best."

"Well, good luck. I'll leave the check and you just stay as long as you want. Give a wave if you need anything, okay?"

"Got it. Thanks."

I sat at my table for about an hour. As always, I took out my notepad and started writing a few topics that everyone interviewed seemed to mention. After a few minutes, I looked at my notepad and saw the following words: values, heritage, hometown, ethics, faith and family. I sat back in my chair and looked around at the diner. I noticed Mr. and Mrs. Miller were enjoying some pie and coffee. I decided to stretch my legs and walked over to them.

"Hello, I'm Elizabeth. I've been talking to a lot of the town's people today for an article I'm writing. It's about small towns in New England and how they're endangered."

"No town endangered here," replied a stoic Mr. Miller, as he took another bite from his pumpkin pie.

"What's your name again dear?" asked Mrs. Miller.

"Elizabeth."

"Oh my, what a pretty name. You know, so many people shorten their name or have a nickname. I'm so glad you use your full name. Why don't you pull that chair over and join us.

Patty, can you spare another piece of pumpkin pie for this lovely girl?"

"Coming right up Mrs. Miller," Patty shouted from the kitchen.

"Now, I heard you are from New York, and you have a friend traveling with you, too?"

"Yes, that would be Max. He's a photographer." I moved my arm to make way for the slice of pumpkin pie Patty placed in front of me.

"Are you married to Max?"

"Oh no. We just work together."

"Oh. You know, in my day, if a lady was traveling with a man and they weren't married, well it would be the talk of the town," Mrs. Miller said with a giggle.

"So, why did you choose our town to visit?" asked Mr. Miller.

"The magazine I'm writing for selected the towns that Max and I travel to. However, I heard there is a factory that is interested in buying some land around here and some of the townspeople like the idea."

"Those people only see the dollar signs. It's these kids today. They want everything and they don't think of the consequences. You know what that factory will bring?"

"Umm."

"Chemicals," Mr. Miller continued to speak. "That factory will bring nothing but chemicals. That stuff will go in the ground and ruin this land. Land that has provided for many generations. After that happens, it will be too late for anything else and then what will these young people say to their kids. I ask you that!"

"I can see your point. Maybe you should address it at a town meeting."

"No need to...I own half the land in this town and it's my land that the factory wants, and they're not getting it. And that's the end of the story."

"Well, at least I can put in my article that there is one small town in New England that is not endangered."

"You can also tell everyone that when they visit from the city they should respect our town. So many of you city slickers

145

come here to 'get away from it all' and then you ask us why there aren't any fancy restaurants. Just drives me nuts, right dear?"

"I have to agree with him on that."

"So, you don't mind if I include your comments in my article?"

"Don't mind at all. Just make sure it's accurate. I hear what they do in those tabloids."

"Don't worry about that. I always print the exact quote. Well, I do have another interview in ten minutes. Thank you for the pie and the conversation."

"It was a pleasure, dear. Be careful on those back roads and be back at the hotel before dark. We don't have street lights out here," caringly advised Mrs. Miller.

"Thanks, I'll be sure to do that."

I waved goodbye to the waitress, collected my things and walked out the door.

I looked at my note pad for the directions to my next interview and slowly drove down the road. The fall season in Vermont is beyond describable. The trees, in their assortment of colors, are like a flickering fire- without the danger. Every curve on the road gives you a glimpse of the mountain ranges and scenes of the farmers' fields in the distance. I made a mental note to take Max here tomorrow before we leave the town. He should definitely get a few pictures of the views from this road. I wondered if the people that travel this road every day see the majestic beauty in these hills, or do they just race home to try and complete all the days' tasks like everybody else in this busy world. 'So many tasks, and yet so little time...how will you choose which tasks to do today?' I said out loud in the car. It was something my Grandpa Frank always said when he saw so many people in a hurry, or making an excuse to end the conversation because they had other things that must be done. I remember sitting with him in Mr. Ferrucci's hardware store when I was ten years old...

"Excuse me, I'm looking for Pedroncelli Construction. Do you happen to know where that is?" asked a strange man, who seemed to be in a bit of a hurry.

"Yes, I know where the Pedroncelli's live. They've been living in Southington since 1938," replied Mr. Ferucci.

"That's great- would you care to share that information with me," the stranger responded quickly.

"Are you doing some building, son?" asked my Grandpa Frank, as he stole a bite from my Three Musketeer bar.

"Uh yes," he answered, as he quickly looked at my Grandpa and then back to Mr. Ferrucci. "Look, I'm in a bit of a hurry. I've got a list of people to see in this town and my deadline was an hour ago."

"I see, that doesn't sound good," answered my Grandpa Frank. "Why don't I show you the way to the Pedroncellis' place. You'll get there twice as fast."

"I don't think so. My car can go pretty fast, but I wouldn't feel comfortable with a kid in the car." He gestured towards me. "Besides, like I said, I have a lot of other places to go today to get the contract. So, how about those directions, sir?"

"Yes," responded Mr. Ferrucci, as he took out a piece of paper and pencil.

"Thank you very much. Have a good day." He quickly walked out the door with the directions Mr. Ferrucci had written for him.

"That guy is in an awful hurry, Grandpa Frank."

"So many tasks, and yet so little time. How will you choose which tasks to do today? Well, that man didn't choose wisely, Elizabeth."

"What do you mean, Grandpa?"

"If that man let me come along, I would have personally introduced him to Mr. Pedroncelli."

"So?'

"So... Mr. Pedroncelli and I are good friends. If I say to my friend, 'this man would like to do business with you', than Mr. Pedroncelli will be good to him. Now, that man is just a stranger and he doesn't even know that my friend knows all the people on his list that he thinks he must see today to get these building permits. Oh yes, that man made a mistake to think he was in a hurry."

"He sure did," laughed Mr. Ferrucci.

"Why didn't you say anything, Grandpa?"

"Because, people like that have little faith. They see themselves as the one in charge. When you think you are the boss, you have little respect for others around you. That man walked in here and thought all we were good for was directions. I bet he never thought we could actually help him with his tasks. It's because he is so busy with his own tasks, he doesn't see all the other people around him...people that may be sent to help him not have such a busy day. Always remember, God doesn't give you more than you can handle. He always sends you help, but you must not be so busy in your own greed to not see the angels. Capisce?"

"Capisce."

"That is good advice, Miss Elizabeth. This world is in such a hurry and then people get old and say 'where did the time go'."

"You won't say that, Grandpa Frank." We started to walk out the door.

"No way, Jose. You like that, now I speak Spanish, too."

"Very funny, Grandpa." We walked past the shops and headed back to my grandparents' house.

'Sorry Grandpa Frank,' I said to myself as I drove down that Vermont road, 'but I really don't have time to stop this time and enjoy the view.' I approached the next turn and found the house. It looked a little neglected, so I assumed an elderly couple was living there. I walked to the front door and rang the bell. After a few more times without an answer, I decided to walk around the property. The owners have a great view of a dairy farm in the distance. There were some neglected apple trees and a barn that had seen better days. As I walked around to the east side of the house, I could see another small house down the road. I decided to go for a walk and knock on their door for some information. As I approached the home, I heard a lawnmower in the back yard. I decided to walk towards the sound of the lawn mower, hoping I'd meet a friendly person.

"Hi there." I approached an older gentleman riding his John Deere lawnmower.

"Hi yourself." He lowered the throttle and slowly drove towards me.

"I was wondering if you could tell me where your neighbors are?"

"Well, this actually isn't where I live. I just cut the grass and care for the place. You see, this home is a summer rental. Right now, I'm getting it ready for the winter. I won't be back here until the spring. Good thing you came out today, huh?"

"It sure is. So, the couple I was supposed to interview, they just rent here?"

"Hell no, the Jamesons have lived in that house over there since forever. When this was a working farm, this little cottage is where the farm hands stayed. Yeah, back then, it was a real fine farm."

"So, what happened?"

"Oh, you know, the same old story. Kids grow up and want to see the world. No one wants to stay in one place anymore, especially on a farm. It's a twenty-four hour a day job."

"That's for sure."

"You grow up on a farm?"

"No, but my mother did, and I heard a lot of stories from my grandfather."

"Oh, I see. So, are you here to buy the place?"

"No, I was actually here to talk to the Jamesons. You see, I'm writing an article."

"Oh, you're that newspaper girl. Yeah, I heard about you."

"At Patty's Diner," I quickly answered with a grin.

"No, at the barber shop. Yeah, Patty's husband is the barber."

"I see."

"Well, I hate to be the bearer of bad news, but Mrs. Jameson passed away two weeks ago and her husband moved to some fancy condo place in Barrington. The kids convinced him to move before winter. That's why I asked if you were interested in buying."

"Yeah, I understand."

"It's an awful nice place and it comes with this cottage and just about 200 acres."

"What would I do with 200 acres."

"Well, they use to have some sheep here. Nothing to raising sheep."

"I'll give it some thought. I really wasn't thinking about buying anything on this trip."

"Well, sometimes the best opportunities in life come along when you have other plans."

"Yes, I know that saying well. Well, thanks for your time. I better get back to the hotel and get some work done."

"You take care now and don't forget about the offer. It's a real fine place."

I returned to the hotel and went over my notes. I lost the Jameson interview, but I could use some quotes from my informal interview with the Millers. Not bad, I thought, for the first day. I left a message for Max and went to the office/computer room for guests. I mapped out the rest of our trip and consulted with my editor's assistant to insure all future couples I was to interview where alive and well. My calculations equaled fourteen more interviews and six towns to explore. My plan gave Max and me enough time to travel back to this small town in time for their Saturday Town Fair. Of course, we might decide to just keep driving back to New York. There was something about this town that made we want to visit it just one more time, before our assignment was complete. Who knows, maybe I would feel this way about every small town on our list. Or maybe near the end of our two weeks, I will be just as anxious to return home and start packing for Monterey.

That evening, Max and I discussed the plan to complete this assignment over dinner. He was really happy with the photos he took in town and liked the idea of returning in time for the fair. He contemplated the idea of taking some more photos at this fair and suggested it might be wise to set-up a little booth. People could learn about the article we were writing and maybe provide their thoughts about their small town. We returned to our rooms early that evening. I watched television for about an hour before falling asleep. The next thing I remember, my alarm was buzzing and the clock read 6:00 in the morning. After showering and packing, I met Max for breakfast and we tossed a coin to see who would drive the first shift. I won the first shift. We were on the road by 8:00 with a full tank of gas and no sign of rush-hour traffic. I was beginning to like Vermont.

Max and I really enjoyed every town on our list. We kept repeating the same comments to each other as we left for our next destination. I can't believe small towns like this still exist. It's nice to see towns where everybody really does know everybody else. This assignment has been really fun, but I would pay anything for a slice of New York pizza.

And so our trip continued along Route 7 and back roads in between. We ate at small diners and a few chain restaurants. We slept in hotels and motels. We had cell phone service in most areas, and almost no DSL service at our hotels. We met seniors who represented the tenth or twelfth generation of residents in a town. We met 'newbie's' who moved to the area, in search of something that represented a time when family and the basic necessities were all that was needed to live, and live well. We passed neighborhoods with satellite dishes and restaurants with plaques that read 'George Washington dined here.'

My interviews revealed people who were more interested in what I believed in, then what I did for a living. Some were hesitant to share their life history, as if to question why anyone would be of interest. Others talked about yesterdays that were in danger of being forgotten, preserved and respected. They all shared a common love for the quality of life they cherished and hoped to pass along to their children and grandchildren. They respected the need for progress, but seemed to place more trust in what has sustained them for the past two centuries. Their reliance on family and friends makes them aware of the importance of human kindness. It has them question how populated areas can leave someone feeling so distant and withdrawn from their community.

Max had a blast taking his photos of the great landscapes in the towns we traveled. He also has a way of relaxing people while taking their photograph, which helped a lot when meeting some of the older residents in the community. They were impressed with this new digital age, and loved to see their picture instantly on screen. Max always relishes in explaining his craft and enjoyed every minute with his part of the assignment.

Before I knew it, I awoke to the last Friday of our trip. I met Max for breakfast and we both agreed to spend the day traveling back to that first small town we visited. We could arrive in the early evening and spend a Saturday afternoon relaxing at the fair. Before leaving, I called the hotel we had stayed at and reserved two rooms. The manager of the hotel, who is married to someone on the town council, also agreed to reserve us a booth at the fair. Max wanted to display some pictures and I was anxious to get a few more quotes from some younger people in the town. By 9:00, we were in the car and traveling south. Everything had gone according to my schedule. Later I would realize, my schedule helped to plan an unexpected event...or vice versa; I guess it depends who you think is in charge of your life.

"So good to see you two again," replied the waitress at the diner. She was carrying a bag of maple sugar candy as she approached our booth. "How long are you two staying this time?"

"Just for the night," I answered. "We'll be in the car bright and early tomorrow...destination home."

"Well, look who decided to pay us a second visit?" It was the caretaker I met at the Jamesons' place. He looked a little different all cleaned up and without a baseball cap.

"Hi there. Good to see you again."

"Have you given any thought to the Jameson place?"

"I plan on driving by it tomorrow morning, on our way out of town."

"Oh, that's too bad. I was hoping someone like you would maybe think of using it as a creative getaway. I know how you writers like the quiet and such to write your world-famous novel," he said with a kind-hearted smile.

"That is a tempting offer, but I'm not sure my check book will allow me to make such a purchase."

"Guess you'll have to keep searching Francis," said the waitress, as she patted him on the back.

"Your name is Francis?"

"Yep."

"Does anyone call you Frank?"

"Nope."

"Oh, just thought I'd ask."

"Really, just thought you'd ask because," he asked, with a lingering tone.

"Nothing really. My grandfather's name was Frank."

"Was he the farmer?"

"No. Although, he did grow grapes, if you can classify that in any way as farming."

"Well, it is growing something. Although, the Jamesons tried growing some grapes, but never had much luck with it."

"So, are you saying there is a grapevine on that farm?"

"Used to be. Ain't much to it now. You'd have to start all over, I bet. I don't know much about growing grapes, just sheep."

"Right, the sheep."

"Well, guess I better move along to the kissing booth."

"Real funny Francis," smirked the waitress. "I better come along to chaperone."

"So, we're stopping at that old farm on the way out of here tomorrow?" asked Max.

"I was thinking about it. Do you have any issues with it?"

"None here. I'll just use up some of my black and white film on the place."

"Great. Now how about packing up our things and buying me some hot chocolate?"

"Sounds good to me."

The next morning, I awoke with a bittersweet mood. I had enjoyed this assignment with Max and meeting new people every day. I also was able to complete most of the article on my laptop while driving in the car. I had some minor changes to make and my closing thoughts, but I planned to complete this on the drive home. I offered to take the first shift while Max slept. He was looking forward to not seeing any sunrises for a while. This quiet time would allow me to collect my thoughts about these past two weeks and mentally develop a rough draft to the close of my article. I always enjoyed this type of writing process. I was never one to just sit in front of a computer and let the story develop. Most of my characters and story lines are complete before I put everything on paper.

Before making the turn onto Route 7, I turned left passed the gas station and down the dirt road towards the Jameson place. My heart began to race a bit and I laughed at myself for feeling nervous. I turned into the pebble driveway and turned off the engine. Max was sound asleep, and I decided not to wake him. I quietly opened the car door and walked towards the front of the house. It's funny how you can tell when a house is vacant. It seems to have lost a certain glow or gives a secret message to the passerby that the walls have no one to protect. This house, however, gave a feeling that it carried a lot of memories and once stood very tall among these hills. I envisioned a time when its clapboards were clean and white and there wasn't a cobweb to be found between the posts on the porch. It was once a house that kept a housewife very busy with beating rugs on the clothesline and children safe from the winter winds. I imagined a farmer sitting on his porch after a hard day's work and asking God for good weather until the harvest.

I opened the porch screen door and gave the front door knob a turn. It opened and I smiled. I entered the home and gave a quiet hello. No one answered. My quick survey of the main room told me I was alone. All the furniture was gone and some spiders had already found a new home in the fireplace. The mantle was made from Mahogany wood. My father would like that. The fancy trim and wainscoting showed much craftsmanship was involved in building this house. I could just picture a cozy winter evening by the fireplace, while reading a book I selected from the collection on the bookshelves by each side of the fireplace. The double windows looked out to the front porch and a neighbor's field for grazing cows. I could see his farmhouse in the distance. Close enough to someone to not feel alone, but distant enough to enjoy the tranquility of a country evening. I walked towards the back of the house and entered the kitchen. The sink had a few Coke bottles in it-Francis' of course. The Jamesons left a chair and a small table so he would have a place to rest while taking care of the grounds. 'I'd have to update the appliances,' I thought to myself. The kitchen was just the right size for a table to seat six. Just enough for a few friends to sit and gossip over wine, while I prepared dinner for my guests. The tile floor was in need of repair and the light fixtures looked like they were bought from Sears in the 1950's. My feet led me to the other end of the house, which I guessed, must have been used as a dining room. It was a bit small, but the sunlight made it feel warm and welcoming. I thought this would make a perfect office. It was close to the kitchen to grab that extra cup of coffee while writing. I noticed there were sliding doors that opened to the front room. The downstairs was like one big circle, how perfect, I thought. I walked up the open staircase. Each of my steps was met with a creak. The banister needed some repair, but nothing a few nails and some cleaning couldn't fix. I touched the walls while walking up the stairs and imagined my family pictures displayed on the wall. At the top of the stairs, I stopped and looked down the hallway. I counted four doors, with a bathroom at the end of the hall. I could only imagine the long lines in this house when all the rooms were filled with children. The bedrooms were all pretty much the same, but the view from each window framed a different picture. The first bedroom had a view of the front yard and the majestic mountains that served as a guardian to the dairy farm in the distance. The next bedroom I entered looked out on the barn. If I stood a short distance from the window, it seemed to create a perfect frame of the old wooden barn. As I walked into the next bedroom, I looked out the window and could see the old dirt road continuing along the path. My eyes glanced down, and I smiled at what I saw. It was the Jamesons' grapevine. Of course, there appeared to be more wood beams with dead vines wrapped around them. I could tell that Mr. Jameson once sat proudly under that grapevine. I even saw a few old wine bottles stacked against one of the poles. I started to think of what my Grandpa Frank would say...leaving a grapevine in such neglect....and then I heard a car door close. I ran to the last bedroom that faced the front of the house and looked out the window. Max had woken up and he was loading some film in his camera. I walked downstairs and out the front door.

"There you are," said Max with a smile. "Are you being nosey?"

"Inquisitive," I answered.

"I'm just going to get a few shots and then we can take off."

"Fine with me. Take your time."

I walked towards the barn and opened the door. Francis' lawn equipment and a few power tools were inside. I started to walk towards the loft when I heard a voice.

"Good Morning."

"Oh, good morning Francis. You startled me. I wasn't expecting anyone."

"Well, I just thought I'd stop by on my way to breakfast at the diner. I was hoping I'd see you here."

"Really."

"Yeah, kinda hoping you might fall in love with the place."

"It certainly is a nice home. I'm sure you won't have any problem selling it."

"Well, I won't have a problem selling the land. It's the house I'm worried about. You see, all these young folks come up here, but they want all those modern gadgets you find in these new houses. They tear down these old places and put up something fancy."

"And what makes you think I wouldn't tear down this place, too?"

"Because you didn't call it a house...you called it a home."

Grandma and Me

Max and I drove back to Connecticut without any stops along the way. I didn't mind. I spent the time working on the article. Max, every so often, mumbled about the nice Italian dinner he was going to order when he returned to Manhattan. When the car stopped, I hadn't even realized we were parked in my parents' driveway.

"That must be some interesting story." My dad opened the car door for me.

"Yeah, I had fun writing this article. I'm almost finished, too. Just have to write the closing paragraph and it's off to the editor."

"Well, it will have to wait until after dinner."

"Sorry Mr. Manciano, but I'm moving along to Manhattan."

"Yeah, he has a date with an Italian restaurant."

"No good Italian food in Vermont?" my father chuckled.

"You can say that again. See ya in a few weeks Liz."

"Yeah, maybe I'll e-mail you from Monterey."

"Gee thanks." Max put on his seat belt and started the engine.

"Careful driving," said my father.

"Will do." Max drove down the driveway.

"How about a quick snack before dinner?"

"I think your mom made some brownies."

"Yumm. The best part about traveling is coming home." We walked into the house.

"Well hello stranger."

"Hi mom. It's only been two weeks." I sat at the kitchen table and cut myself a brownie.

"Well, a lot can happen in two weeks."

"Like what?"

"Like all your aunts causing a commotion at the beauty parlor."

"Yes," laughed my dad. "You certainly have given them a lot to talk about."

"What did I do?"

"Well first," answered my mother, "you took off to Vermont with Max."

"That was work."

"And second, you are taking Grandma Marie to California just weeks after Grandpa Frank died."

"She wants to go. It will be good for her, too."

"I agree," said my father. "But you know your aunts...they have to talk about someone. Right now, it's you and your Grandma."

"How is Grandma?"

"She's okay," answered my mother. "She has a lot of visitors, but I'm sure that will slow down in the winter months."

"Has she mentioned anything about the trip?"

"Oh yes, she is ready to go on Friday. Your mother and I bought her some suitcases and a new outfit to wear."

"Make sure she wears it," said my mother in a lecturing tone. "She has so many nice clothes."

"I will. I already made reservations at two places."

"Make sure you take it easy now. Don't forget your Grandma is a little older than you."

"Maybe I should go see her. Just to let her know I'm back and if she needs anything for the trip. She can tell me and I can go shopping tomorrow."

"She's probably having Sunday dinner with one of her sisters," advised my dad. "But if you're that interested, maybe you should call your Aunts and find out where she is?"

"Oh no. That's quite all right. I'll just stay here and fill you in on my trip." I picked up the knife to cut another brownie.

The next day was Monday and I awoke early. I guess I was used to waking up with the roosters the past two weeks. I decided to put on my sweats and go for a walk. I left a note on the kitchen table advising my folks not to wait for me to have breakfast. My plan was to walk to my grandparents' house, and if the kitchen light was on, I would have breakfast with my grandma.

I walked the usual path- down the hill to the corner, pass the old bank towards the old market, left across the tracks- and there was my grandparents' house. It looked good in the morning light. I noticed some rugs hanging on the clothesline, which probably meant Grandma planned to wash the kitchen floor today. I'm sure she is trying to get everything spotless before she leaves for California. I hoped she wouldn't mind one more visitor today. As I approached the front door, I heard a voice from behind me.

"Good Morning, little Elizabeth."

"Oh, good morning Mr. Ferrucci. You surprised me."

"A nice surprise I hope?"

"Oh yes. Does my grandma know you're coming?"

"She better after all these years. Since your Grandpa Frank and I retired, I have been coming over for breakfast every Monday at 7:30. No reason to stop now, I say."

"No reason at all. You hear so many times when a spouse dies that their married friends stop visiting. I guess it reminds them that their spouse is mortal, too."

"Well, Mrs. Ferrucci reminds me every day how lucky I am that she is still alive."

"Where is Mrs. Ferrucci?"

"She will be coming along. She made some apple fritters. I wanted to come and get the coffee started. That's my job."

"Well then, let's start breakfast." I opened the side door.

"Marie!" Mr. Ferrucci shouted. "Just here to start the coffee. Your Elizabeth is here, too. She must of smelled Mrs. Ferrucci's apple fritters."

"Hello Elizabeth. Glad to hear you made it back safely. Is Max with you?" Grandma walked down the stairs and into the kitchen.

"No, Grandma," I answered, as she approached me and gave me a kiss on the cheek.

"You look thin. Did they feed you in Vermont?"

159

"Of course. They do have restaurants in Vermont, Grandma."

"It's not healthy to always be eating in restaurants. You don't know what they put in the food."

"Well Grandma, I hope you realize we will be eating in restaurants while we're in Monterey."

"Well, I suppose a week away from home-cooking won't be too bad."

"You're only staying for a week?"

"Yes, I decided one week was long enough. Besides, I will be having Thanksgiving here this year and I need to clean the house and do the shopping. It will give you some time alone to help you write that book."

"What book?"

"Don't think I don't hear things. You've been telling your parents you wanted some time away from Manhattan to work on another book."

"Hmm- how about a biography of me?" joked Mr. Ferrucci.

"I'll have to think about that one. How about some coffee?"

"Coming right up." There was a knock at the door.

"Hello Marie," said Mrs. Ferrucci, as she opened the side door with a covered basket.

"Oh boy. I can smell those apple fritters." I rubbed my hands together.

"You just wait," said my Grandma, as she took the basket from Mrs. Ferrucci and placed it on the table.

"So, Elizabeth, you are taking your Grandma on a trip?"

"Yes, to Monterey. I can't wait to show her the Pacific Ocean. And I made reservations at a cute tea room and at a restaurant that overlooks the water."

"Well, it sounds like you almost have the entire week all planned."

"It's just two things, Grandma Marie. When you get there, you can look at all the brochures at the hotel and decide what else you'd like to do."

"Everybody in the mood for scrambled eggs?" asked Grandma Marie.

"Sounds perfect," said Mrs. Ferrucci.

"And of course some bacon," Mr. Ferrucci added, as he walked to the refrigerator.

"Well, there goes my cholesterol level for the week." I said.

"You young people need to worry about that because you don't work anymore. In my day, we worked hard."

"And we walked everywhere," interrupted Mrs. Ferrucci. "I remember your Grandma and me walking two miles to the store and then back home with two bags of groceries each."

"That's right," added Grandma Marie, "and we didn't need to go to some expensive gym like these young people do today. You want strong arms, try beating a rug and mopping the floor."

"Alright. I get it. Actually, I met a lot of hard working people on my trip to Vermont...and a lot of them were young too."

"Well, you can't compare life here to life on a farm." said Mr. Ferrucci. "There definitely is something different about growing up on a farm."

"Remember when Frank talked about moving to the country, Marie?"

"Oh yes, he thought we could find a place that reminded him of the little farm in Italy."

"He never found it though," answered Mr. Ferrucci. "Nothing like a lemon farm in Italy."

"Was he really searching for a farm?" I asked.

"He talked about it when your father was a young boy. But he finally realized it's not where you live, but the people you surround yourself with that really matters."

"Unfortunately, today I think it is a bit harder for young people to find good people to look up to. There is so much garbage on television and so many angry teenagers," said Mrs. Ferrucci.

"Yeah, I'm not sure if I would want to have a child nowadays," I answered.

"Oh, but you must," Mrs. Ferrucci quickly answered back.

"Why? Have you been talking to my mother?"

"If you don't have a child, it will be one less good person in the world. We can't let the bad guys win."

161

"Sounds like something an older man said to me in Vermont. He was worried about all these people coming into his small town and changing everything in the name of progress. He believed if more people spent time educating their children about how important small town values are, they would be less willing to destroy their existence."

"And it just shouldn't be in small towns," added Mr. Ferrucci. "There is no reason for people not to have values in small towns or big cities. In my day, Brooklyn was a safe place, because everybody had respect and pride. Today, nobody cares that their actions have consequences. It's an 'all about me' generation."

"There are a lot of people out there that feel the same way. So many people would just prefer to make life a lot simpler."

"Do they really?" asked Mrs. Ferrucci. "So many of these kids have become so spoiled with these big homes and fancy things. I wonder if they could actually live like their grandparents did."

"Well, society has some influence."

"Oh pissad!" Mr. Ferrucci answered. "Everybody uses that word to put the blame on something or someone besides themselves. People forget that they make the society."

"Amen," interrupted Grandma Marie. "Now that we solved that world crisis, let's have some eggs."

The breakfast was enjoyed while I talked about my adventures in Vermont and the beautiful photographs Max took of the sunrises. After we ate, my Grandma gave me a list of things she needed at the store for the trip. I promised to drop them off that evening, before I returned to Manhattan. I always preferred driving into Manhattan later in the evening after everyone got home from work. The next day, I would spend washing clothes, packing for California and putting the finishing touches on my article. My flight left that evening, but I would arrive in San Francisco just in time for dinner. My mother would say it was a jam-packed day, but I liked it that way. I knew if I waited until the next day for a flight, I would be too excited to sleep the night before. I loved traveling to California and was anxious to get everything set at my friend's house for my Grandma Marie's arrival.

"Welcome to San Francisco. It is a cool 72 degrees with some fog over the Golden Gate Bridge, but still a beautiful place to be. I hope you enjoy your stay in San Francisco and thank you for choosing to fly with us."

"Are you in San Francisco on business?" asked the gentleman sitting next to me.

"No, I'm staying at a friend's house and my grandmother will be visiting me for a week."

"Oh, I just saw you busily writing on your laptop and I figured you had a deadline or something."

"Sort of. I was finishing an article for a travel magazine, but now I'm officially off duty. I can't wait to sit by the ocean and write just for me."

"Oh, so you're also a novelist?"

"I've written a few books, but nothing special."

"Don't sell yourself short. What do you write about?"

"Mostly about family...family sagas. But I'm not that creative. I usually write about people I know. Most of the time my characters are a blend of three or four different people."

"That's the best way to write. Tell me, what are the names of your books?"

"Excuse me," interrupted a lady sitting next to us, who wanted to get by.

"I think we better start walking." I noticed people exiting the plane. "Look, here's my card, if you're that interested, visit my website and let me know what you think."

"Thanks, I'll do that. Say, if you're not busy."

"Sorry, I already have plans." I thought to myself, 'what a jerk. He's just trying to hook up with someone before he goes back to his wife and kids on the East coast'.

I checked in to my hotel and collapsed on the bed. I debated on ordering room service or the hotel restaurant. I looked at the hotel information book and learned the hotel restaurant is open until eleven o'clock. 'A lot different from Vermont', I thought to myself. I decided to take a short nap, shower and eat in the hotel restaurant. I always loved hotel restaurants, because the waitresses are very friendly and always give the best advice.

"One for dinner?" asked the hostess.

"Yes," I answered, as I approached the entrance into the hotel restaurant.

"How about a view of the bridge?"

"Sounds great to me."

"Are you staying long in San Francisco?" We walked to a table in the corner of the room.

"No, I'm actually on my way to Monterey tomorrow. I am house-sitting for a friend."

"Sounds great."

"Yeah, can't wait to pick up the car and go."

"If you're renting a car, ask the lady named Lisa at the front desk to help you. She gets the best rates."

"Thanks," I said, and sat down at the table.

The next morning, I had breakfast and spoke with Lisa about a rental car. She arranged for the car to arrive at the hotel for ten o'clock. I went back to my room and e-mailed my editor the article. There was also an e-mail from Max stating he sent the photos in and everything looks good. I packed my things and went down to the lobby. My car arrived shortly after, and I was on the road to Monterey. I have always enjoyed traveling by car, whether alone or with a friend. The entire road trip to Monterey was filled with beautiful scenery, great music on the radio and a novel with endless possibilities.

I arrived in Monterey in the early evening. I brought in my luggage and then plopped on the couch. I could hear the ocean waves and the seagulls, as I lie on the couch. 'This is the life', I thought to myself. I decided to walk to the local market just down the road and get some food. I bought some hamburgers to barbecue, potato chips, and some milk & cereal for breakfast tomorrow. I would make a trip to the bigger supermarket tomorrow to do the major shopping. I planned on taking the next few days to get settled for Grandma and me. Everything will be perfect for when she arrives on Saturday.

"Well, isn't this lovely!" exclaimed my Grandma Marie as she entered the house. "And look at that beautiful view."

"I'm so glad you like it. I'll put your luggage in the bedroom I fixed for you. It has a view of the water, too. You can leave your window open at night and listen to the waves."

"Oh, Elizabeth. Are you sure you'll come back to New England after staying in a place like this?"

"Well, I'll have too. The place isn't mine and if I wanted to buy something like this, I'll really have to concentrate on writing the world's best novel."

"Have you started writing anything since you've been here?"

"Well, I finished that article and sent it to my editor. But if you're asking about the novel, the answer is no."

"How about a walk on the beach?"

"I'd love to. And I can tell you about an interesting man I met on the plane."

"Oh really, is he cute?"

"Not that type of interesting. Gosh, I think he was at least fifty."

"Oh my, and he was healthy enough to fly in a plane."

"Okay, Okay. My point is, I thought at first he was just nosey, so I gave him my website address to check out my writings. He said he would, but I didn't believe him. However, he did and he sent me an e-mail yesterday."

"Intriguing. So, he is going to buy one of your books?"

"No, not quite. You see, he's not just a regular customer per say. He makes movies and he liked my style of writing. He thinks my family sagas are very interesting and people would relate well to the characters. But there's a catch."

"There's always a catch."

"Yes. The catch is he wants me to write a story that focuses on today's society and the values we all share. He wants to make a movie where people get a feeling of having a common bond with their neighbors. Something that represents we aren't all so different."

"Sounds good to me."

"Sounds impossible to me, Grandma. How are we all alike?"

"You already answered that question when you went to Vermont."

"That was one state and in New England, too. You can't take the people from one part of the country and assume they are all the same."

"Why not?"

"Because you just can't."

"That's funny. I can remember a time when I met people from all over the world and we all shared a common interest."

"And."

"And, your Grandpa and I were on a ship to America. We were surrounded by people who spoke different languages and worshiped differently. We all had one thing in common. We all wanted to choose our own paths in life. I don't think that dream has changed much. Do you, Elizabeth?"

The next day, Grandma and I had an afternoon tea in the quaint town of Carmel. I was so happy to see her smile and watch her eyes light up as we passed the shops and admired the views of the Pacific Ocean.

"I can't believe some people get to see this every day."

"I know. I just love it here. Maybe next time, we can convince my folks to come along with us."

"Oh, wouldn't that be nice. But you know, it would just be nice to have everyone together. It really doesn't matter where you are, when you are surrounded by family and people that love you."

"We were just all together a few weeks ago. You want to have another family reunion?" I sipped my peppermint tea.

"Maybe in the spring and under happier circumstances."

"Sounds good to me. Hopefully, my book will be completed by then."

"So you decided to write a story for that man?"

"Yeah, I just don't know where to start. Usually, I have an idea or some direction for each chapter, but I guess it's just more challenging when I know someone is asking for a specific theme."

"I thought the theme was values. Of course, I like to call it common sense."

"Yes, Grandma. Unfortunately, not everyone shares the same common sense."

"Maybe they do, but some people need more reminders than others," Grandma Marie said with a wink. "I also think these people need to be reminded that they are in the minority."

"Do you think they are?"

"Absolutely. It's just that the good people are sometimes afraid to voice their opinion...like you for instance."

"I'm not afraid."

"Good, then you'll write the book."

"I said I was going to write the book, I just don't know what to write about."

"I thought this man said to write about what you know."

"You want me to write about what I know?"

"Don't give me that look. What is so bad with what you know?"

"Well, I'll be writing about me and everyone involved with me, for starters."

"That's not bad. I know everyone involved with you and I don't see any bad. Besides, if you write the truth, what can anyone say? Maybe some people would have more common sense and values if they knew someday someone would be writing about them, capisce?"

"I capisce. I just have a feeling."

"Good, it's good to write with feeling and emotions. That's the Italian side in you, yes? Good, you use that and you get started on this book. Maybe you can get started while you stay in Southington? It is so noisy in Manhattan; I think you would write much better in Southington."

"I was thinking I would write better in Vermont," I said shyly.

"I knew you were thinking about that place." Grandma Marie put down her cup of tea.

"Remember that house I told you about. For some reason, I just can't get it out of my mind."

"That's a good sign. You know what your Grandpa Frank would say Elizabeth?"

"What?"

"Don't ignore what is in your heart. Too many people don't listen to what their heart tries to tell them. They get scared and just do what everybody else seems to think is right. If you don't follow your heart, you never live your life and follow your dreams. Maybe that is why we have so many unhappy and mean people in the world. They get up every morning and go

167

out in the world and they come home exhausted, but they never live. I remember when your Grandpa Frank would come home from work, change his clothes and then go work in his garden and take care of his grapevine. I would say, 'Frank, aren't you tired?' And your Grandpa Frank would always say there are two kinds of tired, exhausted tired and accomplished tired. He was lucky enough to always feel accomplished tired. That, he would say, is when you know your life has passion."

"Capisce." I raised my cup of tea and Grandma Marie did the same. "Here's to living a life with passion, as Grandpa Frank would say."

"He would probably also say this tea would taste a lot better with a little dash of his wine." Grandma Marie laughed.

"Yeah, I'll have to take some of his wine with me to keep me warm on those cold Vermont days."

"Why not take the grapevine?" asked my Grandma Marie, with a warm smile.

"You're serious?"

"Serious. What good will that grapevine do me? I can't make the wine by myself...and since you are persistent on never moving back to your hometown."

"What is a hometown?"

"What?"

"What is a hometown? It's something Grandpa Frank would always ask me when I was in the Army."

"I remember those phone conversations." Grandma Marie sipped her cup of tea.

"I remember them too..."

"Hi Grandpa Frank. It's Elizabeth."

"Hello Elizabeth. It's so good to hear your voice. How is Uncle Sam treating you?"

"Everything is good. I miss mom's cooking, but I really don't have time to taste the food anyway. You know that Army saying, chew it now and taste it later."

"I see....we don't have that saying in the Italian Army."

"Yeah, I 'm sure things are a bit more relaxed in Italy."

"Well, it is just good to hear you and know you are well."

"How is everybody back home?"

"Everybody is keeping busy. Your Grandma is having Easter here, so of course the house has to be spotless."

"Yeah, I don't think I'll make it home for Easter this year. I'm trying to get some leave for the fall. Maybe I can help you with the grapes?"

"Sounds good."

"What sounds good- me helping with the grapes or not being able to come home?"

"The grapes of course. Look Elizabeth, don't worry about Easter, you just spend the day at your other home and enjoy yourself."

"My other home, what do you mean?"

"Your home with your Army friends. Home is where you feel loved and safe. And I bet those Army buddies of yours take better care of each other than some people in this crazy world."

"Yeah, I know they've got my back."

"Exactly, Elizabeth. In the Army, you are learning that every action has a consequence. It is sad that so many people just think about themselves these days. You have a strong family right where you are. You also have one waiting for you back here in Southington."

"I guess you're right. But sometimes, it's just not the same, you know?"

"Capisce. I feel the same way about my grapevine. Sometimes, Mr. Ferrucci will stop by and help me take care of the grapevine. I love when I drink my wine, and I know it was because I spent the day with my grandchildren tending to the vine or making the wine. It was made with love, capisce?"

"Capisce."

"So, don't be homesick Elizabeth. You make your home wherever you go. Just surround yourself with good people and good wine."

"Good people and good wine," I spoke.

"What was that?"

"I was just thinking how Grandpa Frank ended one of our phone conversations. He said you are home when you surround yourself with good people and good wine," I answered, as I collected my thoughts and returned to the tearoom in Monterey.

"All this talk of wine. I think we should go for a walk to work up an appetite for dinner, with a little wine."

"Sounds good to me." I motioned to the waitress for the check.

Grandma Marie and I spent the rest of the week exploring the sights of Monterey. I was so happy to see her smile and laugh. I knew there must have been times when she thought of Grandpa Frank, but she never mentioned it. We enjoyed a great dinner every night with a glass of wine. And, we ended every night by watching the sunset and talking about my future plans.

"Don't worry so much about the future, Elizabeth. It always comes."

"So, you think my plan sounds good?"

"Is it what you want?"

"It feels right to me."

"Then it is good."

"Are you all packed?"

"Yes. Now, I just have to say my prayers that it is a good pilot and I will be ready for my morning flight."

"Very cute."

"And what will you do in sunny California for the next few weeks?"

"I may play a little golf and make a few phone calls."

"Any phone calls to Vermont?"

"Well, I better make my first phone call to Manhattan. I'm not sure what they will say."

"Will what they say change your mind?"

"No," I answered quickly and with a smile.

"Good. Now I know it is time for me to leave."

"Your work here is done?" I asked jokingly.

"God willing, I'll be working and caring for people until my dying day. And I wish the same for you, Elizabeth." She kissed me goodnight.

I watched the plane leave the airport and fly into the beautiful California sunrise. I knew Grandma Marie was happy to return to her comforts of home in Connecticut. I drove back to Monterey and stopped at a small café for coffee and a danish. I sat outside and watched the waves roll onto the beach. I mentally prepared for my telephone conversation with my boss. I knew it wasn't going to be an easy conversation. However, Grandpa Frank always said if following your passion were easy, there would be no mean people in the world.

"Yes, I know it's a bit sudden, but I finished all my travel assignments. And the monthly articles I can e-mail to you."

"So, you won't be keeping your place in Manhattan," my boss asked during our phone conversation from Monterey to New York.

"I wasn't planning on it. Look, if you still want my monthly articles, I'd love to write for you. But you have to let me know, or I'll start submitting elsewhere."

"No, no. I don't want you to do that. I just can't figure you leaving Manhattan. Are you staying in Monterey?"

"No, I plan on buying a place in Vermont."

"Not in one of those small hick towns I sent you and Max?" he asked with a laugh.

"That was my plan."

"And what do you plan to do up there when it's ten feet of snow?"

"Write, James...I plan to write."

"You can't write in Manhattan?"

"Not when I have deadlines and accepting jobs just to pay the rent. James, my mind is made up. I want to leave on good terms...you've been real good to me...and I wouldn't mind receiving a few assignments now and then."

"When are you coming back to Manhattan?"

"Probably on Thursday. I need to be in Vermont the following Tuesday to close on the house."

"Great. Look everything will be fine. Just stop by the office on Friday, okay?'

"Okay. Thanks, James," I said and hung up the phone.

I spent the remainder of my vacation on the phone with the realtor in Vermont and my bank in Manhattan. I also called Max and asked for some help with my apartment. He wasn't surprised to hear about my plans, but still offered a few words of advice. I've learned that people who are too afraid to try something different are always willing to discuss all the negatives with people who are willing to take the challenge.

I arrived in Manhattan the following week and took a taxi to my apartment. When I entered, I dropped my suitcases and just went to bed. I knew I had to get up early and meet with my boss, James, in the morning. The next few days would be an endless time of packing and phone calls. I never liked moving, although I have done it often. As I crawled into bed, I thought to myself- 'let's make this the last move, Elizabeth.'

"Well, if it isn't the future farmer," said James, as I entered his office in downtown Manhattan.

"Very cute." I sat down in a chair by his desk.

"You know I'm kidding. I give you credit, kiddo. Not many people would be willing to give up a paycheck on such a risky adventure."

"Adventure? I wouldn't call me leaving Manhattan to move into a house while having a nest egg and a job an adventure."

"What's the job?"

"I've been asked to write a screenplay. I plan on using some characters from my short stories and writing a family saga."

"Family saga? Do people still read those things in Hollywood," he said with a laugh.

"I like writing about families and this director thinks it will sell. It's what I always wanted to do, so why turn down the opportunity of a lifetime?"

"Why not do both? Stay with us and write the screenplay for this guy in LaLa land."

"Because I don't have to. I can make a fine living in Vermont doing what I enjoy. I really liked it there and I can see myself living there for a long time. Here in New York, everybody seems to be here for the hope to make something better of themselves. I've already done that and it's time to move on."

"Well, I really do wish you luck, Elizabeth." James shook my hand. "Unfortunately, I'll have to promote someone else in the department to write your monthly articles."

"I understand your insecurities completely," I said as I stood up.

"Insecurities?" James asked with a questioning tone.

"Yes, insecurity. It's what you feel every time you open your bottom desk drawer and glance at that unfinished novel."

"Are you implying you're better than I am because-"

"No James," I interrupted, "I just don't have time to deal with negative people. My Grandpa Frank would always say negative people get that way when they feel life has cheated them somehow. But in reality, life always gives you every opportunity you need; you just have to be ready to accept the challenge. Some people just can't do it, and they try to keep everyone around them feeling as frustrated as they are. You know the saying- misery loves company."

"Well."

"Well, don't call me for an interview." I walked out of his office.

I walked outside with my little brown box of desk supplies and memorabilia. I decided to stop at a coffee house and give Max a call. When I started to tell him what happened, he decided to take an early lunch and talk to me in person. He arrived within twenty minutes.

"I can't believe he just took away your job like that." Max sat down with a cup of coffee.

"To tell the truth, I wasn't surprised. It's business and I wasn't playing the game anymore."

"Yeah, we're just pawns in this crazy world."

"Not me, not anymore. It's not natural for people to have no control over their life. Look around this place, everybody is running around like they are the most important person in the world. If they don't show up for work, then the whole world will fall apart. Remember when we were in Vermont at that café? Everybody was talking to each other and they were talking about family and friends and spending time together. They know each other and therefore care about each other. The only thing James cared about was meeting his deadline so he could look good in front of his boss. I think too many times we try to impress the wrong people."

"Well, I always enjoyed working with you and I think James is an idiot for letting you go."

"Thanks Max. I think I'll be okay. I'm starting to think it's probably best to start with a clean slate."

"You don't get those chances too often."

"What if someone wiped your slate clean? Would you go for it?"

"What do you mean?" Max asked with a bit of skepticism.

"Come to Vermont next summer and find out."

Remembering to Live

"So this is the good life!" exclaimed Max, as he walked towards the front porch of my Vermont farmhouse.

"I like to think so." I put down a pitcher of iced tea and gave him a hug.

"How's life been treating you this past year, Liz?"

"Life has been good, real good, Max. Sometimes I wake up in the morning and can't believe I'm actually living here. I've written more in a year than I have the past five years."

"Hmmm, maybe I'd better join you. I've been so busy with Sports Illustrated, I haven't taken a single landscape photo in months. I was thinking of spending a few days at the Cape after your Fourth of July picnic this weekend. You know, try to get the creative juices flowing again."

"I think that's a great idea, Max. And you can think about my offer."

"Offer?"

"Yes, to join me on a little road trip. You see, I finally completed that children's book I started a few years ago, and now I need some photographs of the United States. So, I thought you and I could do some traveling in the fall. I purchased a Road Trek and I have a route all planned. I have a nice advancement from the publisher to pay our way the next two months, too."

"Sounds like you've got it all planned. Except for one thing."

"What's that?"

"I haven't said yes." Max smiled, as he poured himself a glass of iced tea.

"What's stopping you?"

"Just all those deadlines I have that bring along paychecks."

"Well, just give it some thought. I'm set to leave after Labor Day Weekend, with or without you," I answered with a smile.

"And if you leave without me...what about the photos?" Max asked inquisitively.

"I've asked a few other photographers from the old work place." I smiled and walked inside the house.

"Sounds like a great opportunity, Max," interrupted my Grandma Marie, as she rocked in a chair on the porch.

"Oh, hello Grandma Marie. I didn't see you there." He leaned over and gave her a kiss.

"So, things have been going well for you in the city?"

"Yeah, everything is good. Do you plan on staying here for a while?"

"Just for the summer. Elizabeth asked me to help her with a few things."

"Well, it's good you're keeping busy. You know, I often think of Grandpa Frank. He was a real great guy to talk to."

"What do you think he would say about your dilemma?"

"What dilemma? You mean your granddaughter's offer of the road trip? Well, now...I guess he would say listen to your heart. Unfortunately, my heart doesn't provide the same income that my brain does."

"Elizabeth seems to be doing well."

"Yes, she really fixed up the old place. Looks a lot different from when we saw it a year ago."

"Looks like somebody lives here. Made it a home, you might say?"

"Yep, you could say that."

"Takes a lot of time and passion to make a house a home. Just like living a good life, it takes time and persistence. When you look back, if you did it right, you can smile and be proud."

"I'm hearing some words of advice here."

"Oh, you don't need advice. You're a grown man. But, it's always nice to be reminded of your purpose in life."

"And what's my purpose, Grandma Marie?"

"People always seem to worry the most about the answer to that question. I think maybe they are afraid their answer won't be right. I say, if you answer honestly, how can you be wrong?"

"Good point. I guess, then, my answer would be taking photographs."

"You guess?"

"Well, that's the profession I've chosen."

"If it's your purpose in life, you should answer yes or no."

"Yes or no to I'm a photographer?"

"Yes or no to the question -being a photographer makes me happy."

"I enjoy being a photographer most of the time."

"The key is finding when you are happy being a photographer all the time."

"Well, if we could be happy all the time-"

"I know what you're going to say. The world isn't perfect and no one can be happy all the time. But I think that is the secret of life, to just be happy and take things as they come...be open to opportunity. My Frank and I always saw all the possibilities in life. We were never afraid of what we might lose, because we always knew we would have each other, everything else was just extra. I guess that's the difference with your generation. You all have so many things to hold on to, it gets impossible to let go of one thing without dropping three more."

"Well. It's a more complex world today, Grandma Marie."

"Yes, I wonder how it got that way." She rose from her chair and excused herself.

"Need any help in here?" asked my sister, Rose.

"How about taking out the deviled eggs," I answered, as I looked up from cutting the pepperoni.

"Your kitchen looks great, Elizabeth. You must have spent a fortune fixing up this place."

"Not really. Things are a lot less expensive here compared to New York and Connecticut...and the help is a lot friendlier too."

"So you made some friends?" Rose asked with a smirk.

"I've met everyone in town. I go to the diner about three times a week for lunch and catch-up on the gossip."

"Oh, you're turning into a real Yankee."

"Very cute. Just take the deviled eggs out, would ya?"

"Is your sister teasing you?" asked my mother, as she entered the kitchen.

"No more than usual."

"Your father and I are very impressed with all the work you have done with this place. It looks beautiful, Elizabeth."

"Thanks mom. And thanks for bringing the grapevine last fall. I can't wait to pick some grapes this season."

"Do you really think you'll get any grapes the first year?" asked Max, as he joined Mom and me in the kitchen.

"Of course I will."

"Now I'll have to definitely come back in the fall to check it out."

"Oh, you're coming back in the fall?"

"Well, I've been offered to help on one of your daughter's books."

"What book is that?"

"The children's book, mom."

"Oh, I thought you'd given up on that book. I always thought it was so cute."

"Well, I finally found a publisher who feels the same way," I answered. "So, Max, are you saying yes?"

"Yes, I think I must be crazy, but yes."

"You're not crazy. And, when you come in the fall, bring some of your photographs. You can display some of them in the diner. You'd be surprised how many people visit here in the fall...and with lots of money."

"And what makes you think the owner of the diner will let me?"

"Because you're looking at one of the owners."

"Well now, you've just turned into the entrepreneur!" exclaimed Max. "Who are the other owners I need to speak to?"

"That would be me," answered my Grandma Marie, as she entered the kitchen.

"They got you to invest in this little town, Grandma Marie?"

"They need some good Italian know-how to spice up the sauce."

"And to make the wine," I added.

"You brought your Grandpa's press here?" asked Max. "Now I may stay the whole winter!"

"Everyone will be warm this winter," said Grandma Marie. "I can just see your Grandpa Frank smiling down on us now."

"You really think that grapevine will produce any grapes this year?" asked Max.

"It's my Frank's grapevine. It was planted with love and passion more than fifty years ago. It has been cared for and nourished with time and commitment. Its roots are strong. Frank would say, caring for a grapevine is like caring for a family. If you take time every day to show care and passion, then the roots will become unbreakable amongst life's many storms. It will flourish and blossom anywhere, because it was given love."

On a crisp late August morning, I paused at my desk and looked out my office window. I could see the FedEx truck pulling out of my driveway. I walked towards the window and admired the rolling hills of Vermont. Soon, I thought to myself, the leaves would be ablaze in a myriad of colors. Tourists would be visiting my small town and eating in the café. I hoped the travelers would enjoy my Grandpa's wine. I walked through the family room and opened the front door. There, on the front porch, a package with a postmark from California. I smiled as I bent down to pick it up. I cradled it in my arms and looked up at the sky. 'Thanks Grandpa Frank...for teaching me that freedom is not getting what you deserve. It's having the opportunity to be what you never thought was possible and do what you never imagined could be attainable.'

"Here it is!" I shouted to my Grandma Marie, as I walked towards the backyard.

"What's that?" she asked, sitting under the grapevine with her cup of tea.

"It's my book...the family saga I worked on all winter. It just came in the mail right now. It was sent Federal Express from our producer friend in California."

"Oh, how is he?"

"He wrote a quick note. I'll read it to you." I sat down next to Grandma Marie, under the grapevine.

Dear Elizabeth,

I send you best wishes as I write this note to you. I hope you are well in Vermont and your home renovations are going smoothly.

I was very excited when your book arrived in the mail last spring and read it from beginning to end that same day. It goes without saying, I was not disappointed. Your characters are so honest and, with their flaws, make them so relatable to any reader. I look forward to seeing you next spring, when we start production of the movie. Until then, keep writing!

Sincerely,

Your Number One Fan in California!

"What a nice thing for him to do," said my Grandma Marie. "I'm sure he is a very busy man."

"Yeah, I'm glad I decided to trust him and write the book."

"You decided?" answered my Grandma Marie with a smile. "Are you sure you didn't have a little persuasion from a wise woman?"

"Maybe a little." I pulled the book out of the envelope.

"Oh my, what a beautiful cover. Your Grandpa Frank would be so proud."

"Well, I hope you like what's inside the book, too."

"I don't have any plans today. Why don't you read it to me here. That way, your Grandpa Frank can hear it, too."

"I can't recall the first memory I have of my Grandpa Frank, but I can recall the many Sundays at his home just listening to him speak. He told stories of coming to America with ten dollars in his pocket and his best girl by his side. When he laughed, you could see his stained teeth from all those cigars he smoked since the age of twelve. His face was worn from working outside at the trolley yards..."

THE END

About the Author

Linda Massucci was born and raised in Southington, Connecticut. Her writings reflect the importance of family, faith, values, ethics and always remembering your actions have an effect on someone. Besides writing, Linda enjoys photography, traveling, watching old movies, reading, hiking, golf, walking on the beach at sunrise and spending time with family & friends.

If you'd like to learn more about Linda's other published books, you can visit her author website at **www.lindamassucci.wordpress.com** . She answers every e-mail personally and loves to share her writing endeavors on her blog. Her commitment to living every day with purpose and value is noticeable in her writing style and personal life choices. "My perseverance comes from believing that everyone you meet in life may not always be the people you want to meet, but they will always be the people you need to meet."

Made in the USA
Middletown, DE
19 March 2015